HIGH STAKES AFFAIR

They'd been the Romeo and Juliet of Reno, Nevada: the daughter of a blueblooded attorney and the son of a slightly shady casino owner, passionately in love until their scandalized families put a stop to their summer romance. Now Julia Cassidy was an investment banker, cool and cautious by profession—except in the presence of Marc Castellano. Head of a hot new electronics firm and still smolderingly sexy, Marc might be Julia's next big account . . . or her first big gamble. The fire kindled so many years ago still crackled between them, Julia knew, but did Marc want her back out of love—or revenge? And was their explosive new-old affair worth risking her heart for—again . . . ?

HIGH STAKES AFFAIR

by
JoAnn Robb

A SIGNET BOOK

NEW AMERICAN LIBRARY

PUBLISHER'S NOTE

This novel is a work of fiction. Names, characters, places, and incidents either are the product of the author's imagination or are used fictitiously, and any resemblance to actual persons, living or dead, events, or locales is entirely coincidental.

NAL BOOKS ARE AVAILABLE AT QUANTITY DISCOUNTS
WHEN USED TO PROMOTE PRODUCTS OR SERVICES.
FOR INFORMATION PLEASE WRITE TO PREMIUM MARKETING DIVISION,
NEW AMERICAN LIBRARY, 1633 BROADWAY,
NEW YORK, NEW YORK 10019.

Copyright © 1985 by JoAnn Ross

Ø

SIGNET, SIGNET CLASSIC, MENTOR, PLUME, MERIDIAN and NAL BOOKS
are published by New American Library,
1633 Broadway, New York, New York 10019

First Printing, June, 1986

1 2 3 4 5 6 7 8 9

PRINTED IN THE UNITED STATES OF AMERICA

Chapter One

❧

Julia Cassidy stood in the center of her luxuriously appointed office, unconsciously wringing her hands. The rich oak desk gleamed from years of oil painstakingly rubbed into its surface, and the gold design of the hand-printed wallpaper was repeated in the draperies and upholstery of comfortable furnishings. Lush burnt-umber carpeting absorbed the high heels of her pumps as she began nervously pacing once again.

The carefully created aura of warmth was accentuated by a fire crackling away in the marble fireplace. A vase of gold and copper spider mums echoed the autumnal colors, filling the room with a heady scent that mingled enticingly with the fragrant cedar logs.

It was probably only her imagination, overstimulated by the imminent meeting, but as her gaze swept the room, Julia thought she could detect the scent of money. Old money, and lots of it.

She flinched as she caught a glimpse of herself in the gilt-framed wall mirror. Her hazel eyes were enormous, her pupils dilated with both expectation and dread. With her bottom lip captured that way between her teeth, she looked like an unwilling participant at a séance, awaiting the appearance of an unwelcomed apparition.

5

"The ghost of a lover long past," she murmured.

Her eyes softened as her mind took her on a brief trip back through time. No, that was the wrong choice of words, Julia reminded herself firmly. What she and Marc Castellano had shared never had the slightest thing to do with love—at least on his part.

Her unruly mahogany hair had already begun to escape the confines of its tight chignon, and she moved closer to the beveled glass. Her nose almost touched the mirror and her breath made little clouds on the polished surface as she shoved the curling, errant strands back into place.

"Dumb," she muttered. "Dumb and vain to boot, Julia Cassidy." She rubbed the indentation on the bridge of her nose with a perfectly manicured finger, wondering what on earth had possessed her to remove her eyeglasses. She'd never, in her entire career as commercial accounts-acquisition officer for Silverado Fidelity Bank, fussed so much in preparation for a meeting with a prospective client. And she had certainly never opted for near blindness in the name of feminine vanity.

It worried Julia that Marc had only been back in Reno two days and she was already exhibiting such atypical behavior. Had nothing changed in fifteen years? she wondered.

Her introspection was shattered by the shrill buzz of the intercom and Julia jumped to push the button with a trembling finger. "Yes, Marge?"

"Mr. Castellano is here, Ms. Cassidy."

She drank in a deep, calming breath. Here we go, she silently told the woman in the mirror. "Please ask Mr. Castellano to come in."

As Julia walked toward the ornately carved door, drying her moist palms on the russet skirt of her suit, she wondered how an ice-cold hand could perspire.

"Good morning, Mr. Castellano." Good Lord, he looked as wonderful as ever. Better, in fact, with the stamp of maturity on his dark features.

"Good morning, *Ms.* Cassidy." Marc Castellano's inflection was polite, following Julia's lead, but his black eyes were home to dancing devils of masculine satisfaction.

Julia realized she'd been caught staring. Well, she thought, chalk up one point for the visiting team.

"I'm pleased you were able to come on such short notice," she managed to say despite the definite jolt she experienced as he clasped her outstretched hand. Static electricity from the carpet, she assured herself. That's all it was.

"Your letter piqued my interest. It seemed worth taking some time to see what you're offering these days, Juliet."

At the sound of the deeply drawled name he'd resurrected from the past, Julia jerked her hand free. Desperate to put three feet of polished oak between them, she retreated toward the safety of her desk, failing to notice the low table in her path.

"Oh! Damn." The crack of her shinbone against the unyielding brass was followed immediately by her outcry. Tears sprang to her eyes, clouding her vision as she groped for something to steady herself. Julia got more than she bargained for as her fingers curved around Marc's muscled forearm. As if burned, her hand flew off his gray suit, only to be recaptured. Long dark fingers linked with hers, squeezing momentarily.

For all her carefully acquired poise, she hadn't changed, Marc realized. She was still a walking disaster area. His purpose in coming to Silverado Fidelity Bank was temporarily driven from his mind as her accident triggered memories of others she'd suffered that summer. He found himself drowning in a sea of emotions he thought he'd successfully overcome years ago.

"Sit down and let's inspect the damage you've done this time," he instructed on a sigh, his hand on her back as he led her to a chair.

"Really, Marc, I'm fine," she protested, shaking her head in a negative gesture. Curling tendrils of fiery hair sprang from their confinement, curling down the back of her neck. "It was just such a surprise. The cleaning people must have put that table back in the wrong place when they shampooed the carpeting last night. It shouldn't have been there."

Marc reached out and lifted the table leg, eyeing the deep indentations in the plush carpet. That table had been there forever, and they both knew it.

Was it her imagination, Julia wondered, or were his dark eyes mocking her? She studied his face, her gaze moving to his lips, seeking to detect a smile. Those firm, wonderful lips. She could remember how they felt on hers as if it were only yesterday.

"Still up to your old tricks, I see," he murmured, his deep voice laced with amusement. And something else. Was it anger? Whatever it was vanished so quickly, Julia couldn't decide.

Her eyes met his, bravely relenting to his leisurely appraisal. When he reached out to lightly massage the line at the bridge of her nose, it took every ounce of willpower she possessed not to melt, then and there.

Why did he have to be so damn gorgeous? Couldn't he have gotten fat, with a huge beer belly oozing over his belt? Couldn't he have at least lost his hair? Would that be too much to ask? Instead, Marc possessed the lithe strength of an athlete and his thick black hair was the color of anthracite coal. But softer, Julia remembered. So much softer.

"Still bumping into furniture rather than wearing your glasses." He shook his head. "I'm surprised you've made it to the ripe old age of thirty-two. I expected you to have been run over crossing the street long ago."

A smile took the harshness from his tone, and Marc's eyes were not cruel. "You're the only woman I've ever met who had difficulty spotting a bus two feet in front of her."

"It was a coincidence," she lied weakly. "I broke them this morning before I came to work. I'm far beyond silly schoolgirl vanities, Marc."

Marc decided to let the prevarication slide by. "I'm pleased to hear that. It's nice to know that your body isn't the only thing that's grown up during my absence."

His eyes again studied her soft curves, which could never be hidden by the severely tailored lines of her suit. Her body had been slimmer in those days, her nubile figure only hinting at the woman she was destined to become. Julia was somewhat irked to discover he hadn't considered it a woman's body back then. That certainly hadn't interfered with his enjoyment of it, she remembered, welcoming the surge of irritation that rolled over other, more disconcerting emotions.

"You'll find that I'm quite changed, Marc. And more than capable of handling Apollo's banking needs."

Something flared in the jet depths of his eyes for a moment, a reoccurrence of that fleeting, unnerving sensation she'd detected earlier. But his hooded gaze shuttered as he examined her bruised shin. His fingers were strong, but not uncomfortably rough as he probed the lump that was already forming under her torn nylons.

Marc wondered where Julia had picked up this crisp, authoritative manner. It was a far cry from the passionate young girl he remembered.

"I don't doubt that you're a paragon of the banking

profession, Julia," he replied, unable to resist a little sarcasm, "but you're not exactly poetry in motion." He gave her a crooked reminiscent smile. "You've always reminded me of an accident that was just waiting to happen."

Julia silently accepted the truth of his statement. Whereas under normal circumstances she moved with an easy, fluid grace, there were other times she seemed in danger of careening out of control.

Julia knew she was a study in contradictions. The woman who could quote the latest prime rate at the drop of a hat was also known to have trouble remembering her own phone number. The banker who could instantly put her hands on a file of a remote geographical surveying firm in Kuwait could spend an hour searching her office, attempting to locate where she'd left her car keys this time.

And the cool, collected woman who had lured some of the biggest accounts in the country to this low-image Nevada institution had fires burning deep within her that had only flared out of control with one man. The man who was still holding her leg in his strong dark hands, his fingers stroking her bruised flesh absently as his eyes moved to hers.

There was an instant of heat and Julia was hurled back to that first time, fifteen years ago. No. She wasn't going to allow those memories.

"I think I'd better change my nylons," she stated quietly.

His hands obediently dropped away. "All right."

"I'll only be a moment," she promised. "Meanwhile, I've ordered coffee. Do you still take it black?"

"Black and strong. You have a good memory, Julia."

Better than I want right now, she could have answered. Instead, she nodded as she moved with more caution toward her desk, pulling out the spare pair of nylons she always kept for emergencies such at this.

"I'm well-paid to have a good memory."

"Of course. I should have thought of that." Marc's words, bitten off through clenched teeth, were aimed at her back as she left the office.

When George Stevenson had first told Julia to persuade Apollo Enterprises to open an account at Silverado Fidelity, she had thought her business expertise would overcome any leftover problems she might have with the man who had founded a worldwide electronics firm. But she'd been wrong. There were simply too many undercurrents in their relationship.

Over the years, Julia had come to think of her summer fling with Marc as an impetuous, schoolgirl crush, made all the more romantic by her parents' forbiddance of their relationship. Julia's roots went deeply into the Nevada soil. Since her family's arrival in the state, every generation had boasted at least one attorney, beginning with Judge Patrick Cassidy, who had sat on the bench of the old Genoa courthouse in 1865.

The Castellanos had arrived in the state about the same time as the Cassidys, but Sam Castellano had taken another route to fortune, opening a saloon and dance hall in Virginia City shortly after the discovery of the Comstock Lode in 1859. More than a century later, James Cassidy, Julia's father, was a partner in the law firm of Smith, Bates, and Cassidy, following the family tradition of law. In the same vein, Joe Castellano, Marc's uncle and surrogate father, ran a gambling casino, a venture frowned upon by the elitist Cassidys.

It was that prohibition, plus the intense, bittersweet emotions they'd fallen captive to, that had compelled Marc to call her his Juliet so long ago. And while neither had taken poison, the tempestuous affair had ended with the tragic inevitability it had been building toward that entire summer.

Marc paced the room with pent-up frustration while Julia was absent, his obsidian eyes raking over the rich appointments of her office. She'd done all right for herself, but he'd never suspected that she wouldn't. Julia Cassidy was a survivor, always looking out for number one. It was certainly no coincidence that she not only worked at the bank owned by her next-door neighbor, but dated his son and heir as well.

Marc's only surprise was that Julia wasn't a vice-president by now. He had no doubt that her feminine charms had speeded up her promotions, and it was probably only a matter of time before she worked her way a few rungs higher on the banking ladder and gained a seat on the board.

It looked as if Julia had her future all mapped out. There was a ruthlessness to the set of Marc's mouth as he considered the detours he was about to put up on her fast track to success.

With the obsessive behavior of one who's spent a major portion of his life planning retribution, he'd kept close tabs on Julia Cassidy over the years. While his actions had kept the pain fresh and raw, they had also prevented any softening of his belief that he owed her one. He shoved his hand so hard into the pocket of his slacks that the material ripped and some coins dropped to the floor. He scooped them up, transferred them to another pocket, and was seated when Julia returned.

"Are you ready for your coffee?" she asked, smiling with a professional air that made Marc want to wring her gorgeous neck.

"Sounds fine."

Julia pushed an intercom button and her secretary

entered, her blue eyes alive with feminine interest as she put the tray down on the table and turned toward Marc.

"Will there be anything else?" the young woman invited with a smile.

"That will be all, Marge," Julia snapped, her reserve slipping.

Marc folded his arms over his chest, wicked amusement in the glance he directed toward Julia.

"Thank you, Marge." His warm, baritone voice was a distinct contrast to Julia's shrill tone. "I assure you, everything's perfect."

Marge's blue eyes melted as she backed out of the room.

"Haven't lost your touch, I see," Julia murmured, surprised Marge hadn't curtsied while she was at it.

Marc eyed her over the rim of the china cup. "Neither have you, Julia. I notice you've had my favorite coffee prepared. Unless you serve this to every prospective new client?"

The bold Colombian Armenia Supremo beans were not found in the average neighborhood market and Julia had gone to a great deal of trouble to locate them. But she wasn't about to let Marc in on that little secret.

"I happened to recall you liked those beans. They have such a robust flavor, I thought it was a nice choice for today. The weather is turning colder by the minute. I wouldn't be at all surprised if we get snow before the end of the week."

He didn't answer, sipping quietly on the smooth, aromatic brew of freshly roasted beans. The silence filled the room.

"I hear you've been working on a program to encrypt the electronic funds-transfer network," Julia offered finally.

"I've been doing some work in that area," Marc replied, not expanding on his answer.

The silence settled down about them once again.

"Is it really that easy to divert funds from the network? Every time I go to an American Banker's Association meeting, computer theft is all I hear discussed. But I've never actually met anyone who's been a victim."

Marc set his cup down on the table beside him, leaning forward to address her question, his forearms resting on charcoal suit-clad thighs. His expression was distinctly disapproving and a glimmer of challenge lit his dark eyes.

"There are times I think you bankers are living in Fantasyland, Julia, the way you're neglecting to protect your systems. Think of it . . . four hundred billion dollars are transmitted daily in the United States over proliferating financial networks. Sixty-four trillion dollars a year. If your mind tended toward the criminal, could you let all that money flow past you without reaching out to grab some of it?"

"But the systems are incredibly expensive, Marc. Just to encode one automatic teller machine adds five thousand dollars to its cost. We're in business to make money, not spend it. Besides, the return on breaking into an ATM is relatively low. If all I was going to get was fifty or a hundred dollars, I'd probably just wait and mug the customer after he's gotten his cash. It would be easier than spending all that time trying to decipher his personal identification number."

Marc smiled as he watched her brush an errant wisp of auburn hair out of her eyes, momentarily diverted from his train of thought by the idea of Julia Cassidy mugging anyone. She radiated an air of cool composure that was a distinct contrast to the average street thug. And worlds different from the sexy young siren he'd known that summer.

That memory returned the scowl to his face and brought his resolve back to mind. He wasn't here for idle chitchat.

"Believe me, Julia, the EFT system is as vulnerable to being tapped as that phone." He nodded his dark head in the direction of her ivory desk telephone.

"Wouldn't it take an extremely intelligent crook?"

Marc leaned back in the chair, folding his arms across his chest, and nodded. "Sure, as well as one willing to put the time in to crack the code. You've got a point, as far as it goes, about time and effort. Even to decode one encrypted PIN would take a state-of-the-art super-computer an entire day. But wouldn't you be willing to put in some time if the payoff was several million dollars?"

Of course not. She couldn't imagine doing anything illegal; Julia Cassidy did not even jaywalk. "No, I wouldn't." She eyed him with curiosity. "Would you?"

Marc's only answer was a careless shrug as he smoothly closed the door on that subject. "Who knows what we'd do, Julia, until the situation presented itself? Now, why don't you tell me about Silverado?"

Julia paused for a moment, wishing she could pursue the conversation. But it was time to turn to the reason for his visit.

"I assure you, Marc, that while we're admittedly short on renown, we're extremely long on capital. Silverado doesn't cater to the small investor, so we don't offer a lot of the high-visibility, low-income services of many banks.

"We underwrite stock offerings, place municipal bonds, and invest our own money, but much of our business is generated through high-placed clients who prize our confidentiality. Our major enterprise is investment banking, and we can offer you a range of services geared precisely to your unique needs."

She flipped open a file on her desk, preparing to cite specifics, but Marc had suddenly lost interest in the facade. When her eyes returned to the chair, she saw that he had risen and was standing by the window. When he turned, his expression mocked her carefully rehearsed speech.

"You're in your element here, Julia," he noted as his eyes scanned the room, then returned to observe her with disapproval.

His silent, accusatory stance unnerved Julia, and at the rattling noise she glanced down, mortified by the translucent china cup and saucer shaking in her hands. She placed them carefully on the desk and reached into a drawer for a pack of cigarettes. She took her time extracting the long menthol cigarette, her trembling fingers betraying her nervousness. As Julia inhaled the smoke, she knew that with Marc back in Reno, all her good intentions about quitting this, her single vice, would disintegrate.

But she'd known that this morning when she'd stopped at the newsstand on the corner and purchased the pack of cigarettes, her first in six months. Marc Castellano was still capable of inciting a wealth of unwelcome responses, she realized, watching him warily. Julia damned her decision not to wear her glasses as she was unable to discern his expression from across the room.

The silence eddied around them, a living, breathing thing. Finally Julia decided she *had* to see his face. She crossed the span of carpet separating them, but as she drew nearer, she wished she'd stayed across the room. His expression was not encouraging.

"What exactly do you mean by that, Marc?"

He ran his finger over the soft ultrasuede covering her shoulder. "You've definitely acquired some polish along the way, sweetheart. This office, these clothes, are far more subtle than that handkerchief-sized bikini you waved in front of me that summer . . . but you're obviously still an expert at arranging seduction. These days it just pays a little better, right?"

Julia stared up at him, feeling as if he'd just clenched his fist and hit her in the stomach. Forgetting that her aim was to encourage Marc to open a commercial brokerage account for Apollo Enterprises, forgetting that she'd sworn he'd never know how much she'd suffered from his actions, forgetting that she'd worked incredibly hard to remain as poised, cool, and serene as any investment banker should be, she lifted her right hand, aiming directly for his high, chiseled cheekbone.

There was a shattering sound as the flat of her palm connected with his skin. Startled by her instinctive response, Julia could only stare at her hand poised in midair.

Marc's gaze was riveted on her stricken face. "Feel better?" His tone was filled with cold contempt.

She slowly lifted her gaze from her hand to his darkly shuttered eyes. "Truth?" she asked softly as she lowered her hand.

Although something flickered in the black depths of his eyes, Marc managed to keep his expression inscrutable.

"Truth," he insisted.

"I believe I do. In fact, I think I've been wanting to do that for years."

A muscle twitched at the corner of his grimly set mouth, but still Marc displayed no emotion. "Well, that's one of us with a long-restrained longing out of the way . . . When is it going to be my turn?"

Her hazel eyes widened with fear. "You want to hit me?"

Julia knew he could feel her pulse quicken under his thumb as his fingers encircled her wrist, assuring Marc that he was not the only one affected by these illogical sensations he'd been experiencing since he first entered this office.

"You know better than that, Julia. For a myriad of reasons, I've been wanting to make love to you again for the past fifteen years."

"Marc, please," she protested on a soft sigh. "That summer is in the past, where it belongs. We were kids, but now we're adults. Let's try to behave that way." She shivered a little under the impact of his forthright gaze.

"The feelings I'm experiencing at this moment definitely don't belong to any kid, Julia. And I know that however much you protest, your body is crying out for the same thing. So, for once in your life, forget the damn lie."

"What in the world are you talking about, Marc? I've never lied to you." She took a shaky puff on her cigarette as Marc glared down at her.

His voice was silky with menace, the low timbre more threatening than any shout would have been. "Don't push, Julia. I'm working very hard not to give you exactly what you deserve, but behavior like this makes it damn hard."

"And just what is it I deserve?" she challenged recklessly, squaring her slim shoulders. She threw back her head as she met his furious gaze with an antagonistic one of her own. The air was rife with ill will, their voices arched like the backs of cats.

"This," he muttered after a long, dangerous silence.

Before she could protest, he yanked the burning cigarette from her fingers, grinding it viciously into a crystal ashtray. His dark head swooped down, his lips taking possession of Julia's in a kiss that took her breath away.

There was no gentleness as Marc reclaimed what had been his all along. His mouth ground onto hers and his hands tangled in her hair, destroying the carefully tied-back twist to let his fingers run through the flame-colored strands. Resentment, retaliation, frustration, and a burning male hunger merged into a dark force that seared like molten lava through his veins.

He spread his legs, impelling her hips into his, the sharp line of her pelvis kindling a fire in his loins. His hands moved with hot aggression from her shoulders to her thighs, scorching messages that augmented that of his questing mouth.

As Julia swayed under him, Marc closed his mind to the fact that this rash behavior might very well destroy everything. In order for his plan to succeed, it was imperative that Julia Cassidy trust him. That was the key. If he failed at that, he might as well pack up and return to Palo Alto.

But corrosive bitterness ate away at sanity, even as old, unused passions broke free with the violence of a bursting dam. As Marc's hand moved along the sensitive curve of Julia's spine, molding the lower half of her body to his, thought and reason ceased to exist.

Chapter Two

Shock was rapidly overcome by unwelcome desire as Julia's body responded with vivid memory. Her head swam with erotic scents and tastes, both real and remembered. The green, woody scent of the after-shave assailing her nostrils mingled in her mind with the piquant tang of the evergreens growing on Marc's lakeside lot.

His heady, masculine scent was intensified by memories of sun-warmed flesh her lips had explored as they'd lain by the shimmering waters of Lake Tahoe. The minty taste of his breath, filling the moist darkness of her mouth, blended in her mind with the tang of salt she'd tasted on his bronze skin.

All these things conspired against her in a sensual bombardment of the highest order, overcoming years of bittersweet memories. Julia could no more insist Marc stop than she could escape the ironlike strength of his arms. Indeed, she thought she would surely melt at the fire he inspired in her.

"Marc," she managed to plead against his ravaging mouth, her voice a tattered thread of sound. "Please . . . not like this."

Marc realized through the blaze of passion searing his

mind that Julia had not told him to stop, not demanded that he take his hands off her and get the hell out of her office. She'd only asked that he not force himself on her with such brutality.

Brutality. Judas, he'd never harmed a woman before in his life. Yet there'd been only one who had ever given him provocation. Julia had always been able to twist him around her little finger, he realized bleakly, before groaning his surrender and easing the embrace, meeting her request, as he always had.

His lips plucked tenderly at hers, the tip of his tongue running gentle trails of apology over her bruised flesh. He could feel her relaxing in his arms and her pliant female body curved willingly to fit against his strength. Marc's kisses adorned her face; his body shuddered with repressed hunger as he kissed her temples, her cheeks, her chin, and the dip at the bridge of her nose.

Time held no meaning as he savored her sweet taste. Addicted to the scent clouding his mind, he was drawn like a shipwrecked sailor to the fatal call of a mythical siren. When Julia's tongue slipped between his lips, engaging his in a sensual duel of passion, Marc thought he'd explode from wanting her.

Julia had experienced a moment of fear when Marc had first swallowed her protests with his savage kisses, but now it was as if the world had suddenly started spinning backward, returning her to the time when Marc had taught her what it was to be a woman. What it was to have her budding, responsive body worshiped by such a man. Her arms, which had circled his neck as he'd blissfully gentled the kiss, now moved downward, splaying across his back.

"Oh, Marc," she sighed, her breath wafting across his lips as she rained soft kisses onto his face. "It's been so long."

So long, his mind echoed. Too long. It had been fifteen years, yet he'd never forgotten the way her lips tasted or her satiny skin or the sensation of her warm and welcoming body under his. It was as if she'd seared her imprint into every memory cell of his brain, and no amount of liquor, women, or work had ever managed to exorcise her ghost. Even his unyielding urge for revenge had not dulled the memories of shared pleasures.

Cognizant of the fact that such thoughts would only weaken his resolve, Marc drew back, recalling his purpose for coming here in the first place. Dammit, she'd done it to him all over again! He'd forgone all his intentions and succumbed to the pure glory of touching her, kissing her, loving her.

But, he vowed, Julia was about to discover that their game had never finished; they'd only called a time-out. Still, if he forgot his vow and fell back into her sensual web every time she was within arms' length, he'd end up wounded and bleeding again. No. Not this time, baby, he promised. Not this time.

Marc forced his heated body to respond to his demands, denying the hunger that had flared between them as strong and dangerous as ever. He released her abruptly, plunging his hands into the front pockets of his suit trousers as he silently stared out her window at his own building.

Think about that, he instructed, struggling to regain some thread of coherent thought. Business—cold, unexciting banking business. That's what she's supposed to think you're here for. Finally, after a long, hostile silence, Marc turned back toward Julia.

"You've given me enough information for today," he said brusquely. "I'll be in touch."

Julia had put up her own struggle, attempting to get a

grip on her senses as Marc moved away from her. For that brief, golden time it had felt so good. So right.

"All right," she agreed, mentally giving herself points for her tone of control. She'd be damned if she'd let Marc Castellano know that he'd just succeeded in turning her entire world upside down.

She forced herself to withstand the silent scrutiny of his onyx eyes as she refastened the top buttons of her blouse, which he'd opened to allow himself a taste of her skin. The fawn silk had pulled loose from her waistband, and try as she might, she couldn't stop her hands from trembling as she shoved the hem of the blouse back into her skirt.

Business, the last remaining vestige of her mind cried out in an attempt at salvation. Return this battle to your arena.

"If you have time this week, Marc, I'd like to go over some specific suggestions for your account."

Marc's eyes glittered with anger, raking over the seductress who'd just metamorphosed into a cool, competent businesswoman. At first, the very idea of Julia Cassidy as an investment banker had been unthinkable. But now he realized she was a natural. While in the past she had no qualms about using that tantalizing female body to entice a man to forbidden pleasures, she was now playing for much higher stakes.

He knew Apollo Enterprises was no small fish in Julia's banking pond. The company he'd conceived and built to international prominence would definitely be considered a keeper, and she was dangling all the enticing bait she possessed to hook him and pull him in.

No longer the same flirtatious ingenue he'd known, Julia Cassidy had, in the intervening years, become a consummate professional. She was more than willing to allow a taste, a tempting sample of what she was offering for his account.

Marc knew he'd soon have Julia back in his bed, as planned. This idea was even more provoking when he realized she was plotting the same scenario for her own gains. The unexpected twist added a stimulating aspect to his scheme, turning it into a contest. A contest he had every intention of winning. And the victory, when it came, would be far sweeter for her effort.

"I said I'd be in touch," Marc reminded her. He took his cue from Julia; nothing in his controlled, smooth tone indicated the flare of passion they'd just shared. He turned on his heel and left the office.

Julia watched him go, experiencing an inexplicable stab of regret at his brusque departure. Her gaze moved to the mirror, taking in her disheveled appearance. Her hazel eyes were suspiciously moist, her lips swollen and pink. Errant strands of hair framed her face in wavy fingers of flame, and a sprinkling of freckles graced the bridge of her nose, visible due to her alabaster complexion.

Her professional image had been absolutely shattered. Whatever else she did about Marc's return to Reno, Julia knew she had to turn his account over to someone else. Because if there was one thing she was sure of, it was that she was no more capable of controlling herself around the man than she'd been at seventeen.

The rain had stopped, but storm clouds lingered on Marc's rugged countenace as he drove along the wooded highway toward the California side of Lake Tahoe.

Damn her. She'd done it to him again. He no longer loved her. He hadn't since that night she obeyed her father's demands and gave him up without so much as a backward glance. But she could still create instant havoc in every nerve of his body. Getting even with Julia Cassidy was probably going to be the most difficult thing he'd ever accomplished. With the erotic assault she could deliver to his senses, Marc decided it was right up there on a par with piloting the space shuttle.

As he reached his house, Marc cut the engine, not moving from the car as he stared out into the mist-mantled pine forest. He loved this place. He'd traveled a great deal over the years, but he'd never found any spot as beautiful as the unspoiled scenery of this lakeshore. Surrounded by the magnificent, snow-capped peaks of the Sierra Nevada mountains, the waters of the alpine lake were a deep Mediterranean blue. To Mark Twain, Lake Tahoe had been "the fairest picture the whole earth affords." To Marc Castellano, it had always been home.

Expelling a frustrated breath, he leaned his forearms on top of the steering wheel and stared out the windshield. The trees were shrouded in a thin silver veil of rain that had begun again, the dull and leaden sky matching his mood.

As he watched the slanting gray curtain of rain stream against the glass, Marc forced his mind to return to the initial purpose of his visit to Julia's office. He hadn't been at all surprised to receive her letter inviting him to discuss the advantages of doing business with Silverado Fidelity. That had been precipitated by a press release he had sent to George Stevenson, Julia's boss, alerting the bank president of Marc's intentions to move his corporate offices to Reno.

Then, with the subtle manipulation of a chess move, he'd added a handwritten postscript to the formal announcement, asking if Julia Cassidy was still an officer at the bank. As he'd expected, that little postscript had prompted an invitation to discuss Apollo's banking needs. It had all seemed so easy, in theory. But he had never counted on the jolt Julia would deliver to his senses.

"What now?" he asked softly. "What the hell do I do now?"

"Julia, for the last time, you're the perfect person to handle the Apollo account. I don't think we have anything further to discuss."

Julia expelled an exasperated sigh, the air stirring her light fringe of coppery bangs. She was seated in an office decorated in much the same style as her own; George Stevenson's, however, was a great deal larger, befitting the president and chairman of the board of Silverado Fidelity. They'd been going around and around about Marc Castellano and his damn company for the past hour and she was growing more frustrated by the moment.

"George, I appreciate your faith in my abilities, but believe me, Marc Castellano is Sicilian right down to his fingertips. I don't care if he *was* born right here in Nevada, the man will never accept a woman banker. I'll just end up blowing the entire deal." She smiled, a coaxing expression that she pulled out only when she was in the most desperate straits. "Besides, this would be the perfect opportunity for Charles to get his hand into the actual day-to-day activities of this bank."

George leaned back in his chair, buying time to phrase his answer as he pulled a pouch of tobacco from his desk drawer. He filled the pipe and tapped the loose tobacco down, the activity taking longer than usual.

Charles was a sore spot. George had been too busy building the bank's assets to take an interest in his son's early development. That had allowed Charles' character to be shaped by his mother, an engaging butterfly of a woman. A charming hostess, a witty conversationalist, Honey Stevenson was able to discuss the latest trend in modern art or interior decorating for hours. George had heard his wife deliver a five-line synopsis of this year's Pulitzer Prize novel, diluting whatever story was involved into a banal description whose initial message was completely lost in the telling.

If she'd been born with the talent to understand human behavior or motivation, Honey successfully repressed the troublesome ability. Thought made one's forehead wrinkle, and everyone knew the tragedy of that.

The mistake George had made in not taking his son under his wing earlier had created a male clone of Honey. Handsome, witty, a marvelous dancer and expert sportsman, Charles lacked a certain strength George had hoped for—expected, really—in his son. While Charles possessed the ability to gain his own way, it was in a more manipulative manner than his father appreciated. He'd been grooming his son to take over the presidency of the bank when he retired, but at this rate, George figured he'd have to stay in this chair well past his one hundredth birthday.

It was, he considered as he puffed on his pipe, not at all like Julia to want to turn something as important as the Apollo account over to Charles. George knew his son had proposed to Julia on more than one occasion, and while she'd never accepted, she seemed genuinely fond of Charles, shielding him in much the same manner all women seemed prone to do. She knew this account was way over his head.

"Julia, you're an intelligent woman," he stated, brushing at the ashes that fell onto his slacks. "A damn intelligent banker, too," George continued, eyeing her with an admiration that had nothing to do with her obvious feminine appeal. "You're quick, you've got an instinctive business sense that borders on prophecy, and you're one

of the gutsiest negotiators I've ever seen. For the past
nine years I've watched you lure businesses into
Silverado that the guys at Chase Manhatten would sell
their souls to have on their client list."

"Thank you, George," she murmured.

It was not often that George Stevenson passed out
compliments. The last one Julia recalled receiving was at
last year's Christmas party, and at the time he'd seemed
more interested in her strapless white crepe gown than
her financial skills. She wondered idly if he'd been at the
brandy again.

"And that's why," he concluded, abandoning the time-
consuming effort of keeping the pipe going and discarding it in the ashtray, "I can't understand why you're
suggesting handing Castellano's account to Charles."

George shook his silvery head as he thought about his
only son. "That Sicilian would eat the boy alive and spit
him out before breakfast. My son is, regrettably, no
match for the man. As you well know, Julia."

Julia stifled a sigh, knowing it was the truth. She liked
Charles. He was fun, charming, debonair, and never
made her feel threatened, although he'd repeatedly proposed everything from a weekend at Squaw Valley to
marriage. But no, easygoing as he was, it would be folly
to send him up against Marc.

"Why don't you have one of the officers handle Apollo
Enterprises, then?" she suggested. "Or you could do it,
George." Her hazel eyes lit with hopeful gold sparks at
the thought and she leaned forward in the leather chair,
placing her palms on his desk. "How long has it been
since you've gotten actively involved in acquiring a new
account. I bet you'd love it."

George laughed, shaking his head in mute frustration.
As her enthusiastic encouragement brightened her face,
he studied Julia with the eyes of a man, rather than a

banker. Suddenly he understood the motive behind Castellano's imperious phone call this morning. The man wanted her. Not only that, he was willing to bring along millions for payment. Ah, he thought, things were definitely going to get interesting around here. Perhaps it was his age—a belated midlife crisis, or maybe simple boredom—but George found himself looking forward to watching the fireworks.

"I'm too old for shadow-dancing with Marc Castellano, Julia. You're closer to his age. Didn't you two know each other when you were kids?"

Julia suddenly wished she hadn't left her cigarettes on her desk. What she wouldn't give right now for a chance to utilize some of those stalling tactics perfected by George Stevenson.

"Not really," she hedged, taking a sudden interest in her peach-tinted fingernails. "I graduated from high school the same year he graduated from college. The four-year difference was enormous at that age."

"At that age, probably," he agreed. Julia was relieved when he began fussing with the pipe again and knew he'd missed the distress that had flown across her face at the strange track the conversation had taken. "But of course, now it's nothing."

"I suppose not," she agreed briskly. "Not that it matters. The point is, George, he doesn't want to do business with a woman."

She watched as he took out a felt pipe cleaner and jammed the fuzzy yellow wire into the stem of his pipe. George's blue eyes, when they rose to hers, were bright with insinuation. Having put her glasses on soon after Marc's departure, Julia couldn't miss the gleam.

"Did he tell you that?" George inquired, banging the pear-shaped briar bowl of the pipe into the ashtray to dislodge the tobacco.

For one brief instant, Julia was tempted to lie. But she couldn't do it. "Not in so many words."

"I shouldn't imagine he would." George held the pipe up, peering into the long narrow stem as he twisted the pipe cleaner with practiced movements.

"Why is that?" she asked, unable to stand the lingering silence a moment longer.

"Because I received a call from Castellano about you."

Moving her gaze to his hands, she pretended grave interest in the pipe cleaning. "Already?"

Oh, Lord, what had Marc told him? Had he told how she'd practically flung herself into his arms? Had he revealed that she'd actually slapped a prospective client? Had he, heaven forbid, brought up that summer so long ago? Is that what had made George ask about it?

"He called me at home this morning."

"This morning?" Before he'd even talked to her? Why?

"This morning. At six o'clock, before I'd even had my coffee," he grumbled. "Someone should tell that guy about bankers' hours. That they don't begin at dawn."

"I'm sorry," Julia murmured, wondering what possessed her to apologize for Marc Castellano, as if she had control over the man's behavior.

"I don't know why you should be," George returned blandly. He refilled the pipe and began again. With a satisfied expression on his face, he leaned back in his chair, puffing contentedly, eyeing Julia. "In fact, you should be walking on air. Castellano explained that you two were old friends and that if he decides on Silverado, you're the only person he'll allow to handle his account. I'd say congratulations were in order, Julia."

"Congratulations for what?"

Julia was saved from answering George's startling proclamation by the male voice behind her. Turning in the chair, she gave Charles Stevenson a sincere, grateful smile. "I thought you were in Carson City."

"I was," he answered, ignoring his father as he took hold of her shoulders and kissed her cheek. "But I wouldn't miss an opportunity to take the state's loveliest banker out dancing . . . Hello, Father," he said belatedly, eyeing the older man over the top of Julia's head.

Julia attempted to shake herself free of his light embrace, wishing Charles wouldn't treat her in such a personal manner in front of his father. She didn't like familiarity in the office; this was a place of business, after all.

Ha! she lashed out at herself. It had been a place of business this morning as well, and she'd done a lot more than permit a light peck on the cheek from Marc. She seemed to operate under a double standard—one set of rules for Marc Castellano and another for the rest of the world. But hadn't it always been that way?

"What's happening tonight?" she asked, an errant thought roaming about in her mind that she really should know.

Charles' blue eyes widened momentarily, affirming her nagging worry. "Don't tell me you've forgotten? I never will understand you, Julia. You have a mind like a steel trap for banking but can't remember a single personal thing to save your life."

He pressed his lips together in a gesture of frustration and Julia knew it was a constant source of irritation that she couldn't remember their dates. She didn't do it to hurt him. It was just that she possessed a very compartmentalized mind and personal memories did not achieve top priority. Except for Marc, and she refused to consider him right now.

"I really am sorry, Charles," she said softly, forgetting

her vow about proper business behavior as she placed her hand on his sleeve in a placating gesture. "I've had so much on my mind."

"Julia's in the process of bringing in the Apollo account," George informed his son.

She stifled the tinge of irritation she felt as Charles' smooth forehead furrowed in labored thought. "Apollo? Name rings a bell."

Didn't the man ever do his homework? Julia thought. Apollo Enterprises was reportedly leading the world in creating computers with artificial intelligence. Not simple robots, but androids capable of independent thought. For a moment she disloyally considered that one of Marc's creations might actually possess more intelligence than Charles, for all his charming witticisms.

"Computers," George stated dryly, casting a glance toward Julia that asked if she really still wanted to hand the Castellano account over to this man. "Marc Castellano."

"Ah." Charles snapped his fingers as he placed the company and the man. "Castellano. Casinos, right?" He paused, eyeing Julia with scant approval.

"Darling, I know you're ambitious, but do you think it's wise to bring such money into the bank? Lord knows where it's come from."

"I think you've been spending too much time gossiping at the club, Charles," she retorted with a flash of temper that made Charles' blond brows arch upward in surprise. She rose, making her way to the door. "I've got to get back to my office," she lied. "I'm expecting an overseas call."

The air in her office still seemed to vibrate with Marc's presence as Julia slipped her pumps off underneath the desk and curled her feet under her. Lighting a cigarette, she swiveled slowly in her chair, blowing a series of smoke rings up toward the ceiling. She couldn't remember a day ever lasting as long as this one.

"Hey, Julia, don't be angry. You know this town— gossiping about the Castellanos is an accepted pastime. Like remembering when the lake was crystal-clear and there were no fast-food restaurants ringing the perimeter."

Julia forced a smile for the tall blond man standing hesitantly in her office doorway. Charles was right, of course. He'd meant no harm; the Castellano family had been the subject of conjecture for as long as she could remember. But she couldn't help recalling those long, heated outbursts of passionate denial Marc had shared with her that summer, furious that he was not judged on his own behavior. It had always seemed ironic and more than a little hypocritical to Julia that, for an area that thrived on the money brought in by gambling, there were so many individuals, her own family included, who looked down on the profession.

"That's all right, Charles," she sighed, stubbing out the cigarette. "I was just irritated that you didn't think me capable of discretion where the bank is concerned."

He perched on the edge of her desk. "I didn't think that at all. But Dad explained that you've had a rough day, so I'll let it drop."

"Thank you. And your father's right. I've had a long day and can't wait to get home, soak in a hot bubble bath with a glass of wine, and crawl into bed before my alarm clock makes it to double digits."

"You still haven't remembered, Julia."

That's right. He was home from his meeting at the state offices in Carson City for something important. She recalled the conversation in his father's office. Had he ever told her?

"I'm being installed as president of the country club tonight, Julia. Surely you haven't forgotten that?"

She had. "Pick me up at eight," she instructed with a sigh, knowing that she sounded sulky, but not bothering to alter her tone.

"Eight it is, sweetheart," he agreed, sliding off the desk. "And later we'll discuss our future."

He was gone before she could answer. Julia removed her glasses and rubbed her hand over her eyes, feeling a headache coming on. That's all she needed, yet another attempt by Charles to convince her that marriage between the two of them would be an idyllic, constant state of nirvana.

There were times Julia had to steel herself to survive a simple conversation with Charles, despite her fondness for her longtime friend. The idea of facing the man over a breakfast table every morning was definitely unappealing, let alone facing a shared bed with him every night.

Why, oh, why, had he picked this time to press his case again? Julia exhaled a long sigh, flipping open the Apollo file and forcing herself back to work. But she might as well have been attempting to read Sanskrit as the notations and figures kept blurring together to form the darkly handsome visage of Marc Castellano.

"Damn," Julia muttered, slamming the manila file shut once more and stuffing it into her desk. She slipped on her shoes and left her office, not hearing Marge's cheery farewell.

As she pulled her compact Dodge Colt out of Silverado's parking lot, Julia realized she's forgotten to replace the worn windshield wipers. The summer sun had hardened the rubber and she'd been reminding herself since August to buy new blades. They brushed against the glass, the metallic scraping seeming to punctuate each of the day's failures.

Her headache intensified as she strained to see the roadway through the thick sheet of water distorting the glass. Nothing had gone even remotely well since Marc Castellano's appearance in her office that morning. And still to come was a boring dinner dance at the club, followed by yet another proposal by Charles. Not only had this been an incredibly long day, it was looking as if things were going to get a hell of a lot worse before they got better.

Chapter Three

❦

"I don't understand," Charles complained as he walked Julia to her front door. "We're both old enough to know our minds. We've known each other forever; we dance well together, like the same shows, read the same books. What else do you want?

"I want you to be my wife, Julia, but I don't know how long I can keep waiting for you to change your mind."

"That's the point, Charles," she argued softly. "I'm not going to change my mind."

"We're perfect for each other. You can't deny that."

"I can, Charles. I've been denying it all night. We're good friends. But we both know there's an important part of our relationship that's missing."

"Now you're talking about sex," he grumbled. "God knows, Julia, that's not *my* fault. I've done everything but beg, and I'd probably do that, if I thought it would work." He eyed her balefully. "It wouldn't, would it?"

"No." Julia smiled a soft, apologetic smile at his fervent declaration. "It wouldn't. I'm sorry, Charles. But you really do need to get on with your life. Write me off as the crazy woman who didn't know a terrific man when she had one."

He squared his shoulders in the cream-colored dinner

jacket. "I don't suppose you'd like some company for a while?"

"I'm sorry," she turned down his suggestion gently, "but I've got a busy day tomorrow. George wants me to try to get Apollo Enterprises all tied up."

"Castellano," he muttered under his breath. "I'm getting damned tired of that guy already. My secretary's useless. She keeps watching the door for him to walk by. Legal's just as bad. I walked in there today and said hello to Maggie, and you know what she said to me?"

"What?"

"*Buon giorno.*"

Julia dissolved into giggles, imagining the stern, matronly woman lapsing into a romance language. "You're kidding."

"I wouldn't make a thing like that up, Julia. I asked her where the hell she thought she was, Rome?"

"And?"

"She apologized, explaining that she'd been listening to Berlitz tapes, since she might have to translate Italian. I know what Italian she's talking about, and she damn sure isn't interested in his legal briefs."

"Maggie's a very dedicated, hardworking attorney."

"Sure. But think of how many Arab clients we have. Have you once heard the woman practicing her Arabic?"

"No. But they always bring along their own translators."

"You're forgetting," Charles replied as his hands circled her waist, "that Castellano probably doesn't even speak Italian. He grew up here, the same as we did."

As his lips covered hers in an undemanding kiss, Julia considered that she could never forget Marc Castellano grew up in Reno. Just as she'd never forget a single thing about him. Including how his kisses stirred her blood, something Charles simply could not do, no matter how strong his intentions.

"Are you sure I can't come in?"

"I'm sorry," she repeated firmly. "I really do have a long day ahead of me."

"With that gambler," he grumbled, releasing her to shove his hands into his front slack pockets.

"No, with that computer scientist," she corrected firmly. "And if you're going to begin looking into families, I'd be careful," Julia warned, moving to her front door. "Because we have an awful lot of investors who wouldn't stand up to close scrutiny. We all can't trace our roots back to the *Mayflower*."

He took both her hands in his. "I don't want to fight with you, Julia. Let's let it drop, okay?"

Charles lifted her fingers to his lips and Julia lashed out at her unruly mind, which insisted on comparing his unstimulating touch to Marc's. She opened her door, entering the narrow foyer.

"Good night, Charles," she called after him, leaning with a weary sigh against the door as she shut it.

"*Grazie.*"

Stunned by the deep tones of Marc's unexpected voice, Julia turned on the light, staring at him lounging casually in her floral wingback chair. And was that the cognac she kept hidden away for special occasions he was drinking?

"What are you doing here?"

"I told you I'd be in touch."

"That was at the office. And you were talking about business."

"That's right, and now I'm talking about pleasure."

"How did you get in?"

He shrugged. "It wasn't so difficult."

"You didn't break in?" Julia gasped, her eyes widening with disbelief.

"Of course not. You forgot to lock your door." He grinned. "For a woman with such a gorgeous head on her shoulders, you're incredibly absentminded. Tell me, Julia, if I bring my business to your bank, will you treat it with the same disregard you do your own life?"

"I manage to keep my work separate from my personal life," she assured him aloofly. The electricity was arcing between them once again and Julia was amazed the entire room wasn't bathed in a fluorescent glow.

"That will be difficult in our case," he suggested, "since we both know our personal relationship will be consummated long before our lawyers get the papers drawn up for our professional one."

"Speaking of lawyers," she retorted, "I know one who's taking a crash course in Italian. Why don't you try out that Sicilian sex appeal on her?"

"Too easy," he returned smoothly. "I prefer a challenge. And by the way, I do speak Italian."

"Eavesdropper! You were listening to my conversation."

"It was hard not to. You left the front window open, too." He shook his dark head with a gentle chiding. "You're going to wake up one of these mornings covered in snow, sweetheart. Maybe you should keep me here to protect you from freezing to death in your sleep."

"I would have remembered to close the damn window," Julia shot back at him. "And I know you speak the language, Marc. Some of your poems were written in Italian. Why did you thank me?"

Now she'd done it. She'd admitted she remembered him that well. Next she'd be telling him she'd read his poems again last night.

It gave Marc a flush of masculine pride to know that

Julia remembered those poems so clearly. He wanted to know when she'd last read them. Where she kept them. Were they tied with a satin ribbon, tucked away beneath the lacy confections that had always made undressing her such a treat?

"Marc?"

Her soft voice broke into his sensual thoughts and he jerked his mind back to the conversation. "Thank you? You mean when you came in?"

She nodded.

"For defending my honor with your society playboy. It felt good, Juliet. So very good."

Julia's defenses crumbled as she moved across the room, sitting on the carpeting by the chair. She rested her head on his knee for a long, silent time, then lifted her soft, serious gaze up to his.

"I've never believed any of the stories, Marc. And I've never let anyone repeat them in my presence."

She looked so lovely, so sincere, and so incredibly vulnerable that Marc felt suddenly light-headed with unaccustomed indecision. He'd planned this evening for so very long. Planned to weaken her defenses, plotted to seduce her, schemed to make her need him the way he'd needed her.

He'd kept that plan in front of him like his private cache of gold at the end of the rainbow. But now—now he was becoming inexorably trapped in a web of his own making. Because those liquid eyes fired with a golden flame were beginning to hold him prisoner all over again.

"Julia, you've had a long day. I'd better be going."

"Don't go . . . not quite yet," she whispered, looking up at the face that was so incredibly handsome it took her breath away, even after all these years.

His hair had fallen over his brow and Julia reached up to push back the errant ebony lock. His eyes were dark, the color of a robust cup of his favorite blend of coffee, and his high cheekbones were so perfectly formed they could have been sculpted by a master craftsman. His firm straight nose led to full, sensual lips that she longed to feel at all her tingling pulse spots. It was a face that belonged stamped on a Roman coin and it was here in her living room, eyeing her with desire.

"You wore your glasses tonight," he observed, reaching out to tuck a strand of coppery hair behind her ear.

"I always do. I tried contacts, but I couldn't wear them."

"You didn't wear them today at the office." He gave a gentle tug on her small pearl earring.

"I wanted to look smashing for you," she admitted softly. "To show you how nicely I'd grown up." *And to show you what you'd passed up,* she added to herself.

"You certainly succeeded in that." His attention was still directed to her ear as he played connect-the-dots with the slight sprinkling of freckles. "It was all I could do not to ravish you on your fancy, custom-made conference table."

"I know," she murmured, her voice half-honey, half-smoke. "I felt the same way." Julia was compelled into the admission, her voice trembling with pent-up desire.

"Truth?" he inquired in a gritty voice.

It was a game they'd played that summer. Well, it had started out as a game. But before they'd finished, they'd learned more about each other than either had ever thought possible.

"Truth," Julia agreed on a whisper as the innocent touch at her ear kindled fires deep within her. "Because despite your success and my career, despite all the intervening years, nothing's changed, Marc. We're like fire meeting a flammable vapor—the explosion is inevitable."

Her voice wavered and she turned her head away, but Marc caught her chin in his fingers and returned her gaze up to his. With his left hand, he reached down and slowly, solemnly, removed her glasses, placing them on a table beside the chair.

"I don't remember you being so honest with yourself, Julia," he said softly, his dark eyes searching hers to determine if she was actually being truthful about her feelings.

"I've had quite a few opportunities to look at myself without rose-tinted lenses, Marc. And I've actually grown to like what I see."

"So do I." He lowered his dark head with a deep sigh of masculine surrender. "And the view gets better and better."

Julia delayed the kiss, holding Marc's head between her palms. "Why?" she whispered.

"If you're asking why we're drawn to each other like this, Juliet," he whispered, "I'll be damned if I know. I've asked myself that question a million times."

"Oh, Marc . . . this is hopeless."

"Probably," he agreed, his voice unnaturally husky and roughened with desire and a certain anger. His hands rubbed up and down her arms. "It always was. But it was damn good too, you can't deny that."

Julia breathed a soft sigh as she felt herself succumbing to the overwhelming attraction neither of them seemed able to fight. Marc's hand cradled her chin, lifting her face for his kiss. Her lips parted in anticipation as he slid off the chair to join her on the carpet, gathering her into his arms.

She was surprised to find his kiss undemanding; he drank from her lips tenderly, lovingly. Julia could taste the cognac he'd helped himself to while waiting, and it was as if the expensive liquor was conspiring with his firm lips to make her drunk.

Her fingers played with the ebony strands of hair brushing his snowy-white collar, and a small intake of breath invited the tip of his tongue to venture forth. As it probed delicately, brushing against her teeth, Julia heard a soft moan and realized it came from deep in her own throat.

She pressed against him, her breasts crushing against his hard chest, her legs tangling with his. Her hands moved against his back, as if she could meld their bodies into a single unity by sheer pressure alone.

Julia wondered at this force that had always made her respond so impulsively to him. How was it that Marc Castellano, with only a look, or a kiss, could make her feel more womanly than she'd ever felt in her thirty-two years? How was it that one man's kisses were merely pleasant while another's drove her over the edge of sanity? Julia knew nothing of time, nor place. Only this spiraling, overwhelming need.

Marc's soft, coaxing lips plucked and teased, promising so much more. Julia knew she should pull away from his wonderfully sensuous lips and insist he go home now, before things spiraled completely out of control. Soon, she promised herself, flinging her arms around his neck and pressing her mouth more firmly against his. She kicked off her shoes as her legs tangled with his.

"So womanly," he murmured, his hands heating the material covering her breasts. "You've definitely grown up, Juliet."

Marc's voice drifted off as he folded the material down to her waist. Only the wispy nylon bra was between her skin and his roving lips, which were caressing the swell of creamy flesh at the top of the lacy black cups. His hands moved to her back, unfastening the catch with a nimble, deft movement. Her skin gleamed like an iridescent pearl and Julia watched entranced as his dark head lowered, his lips lightly caressing her flesh.

"You're so beautiful," Marc murmured as his kisses blazed a trail over her body. "And you taste so, so sweet, Juliet. I've never forgotten the taste of you."

His hands moved over her curves, urging Julia into more intimate contact, demonstrating she wasn't the only one affected by their slow lovemaking.

"I want to feel you, Juliet. It's been so damned long." His lips nuzzled in the warm shadow between her breasts, inhaling the whispery scent of sandalwood and flowers of her perfume. He was like an alcoholic, drawn to the essence of her with an uncontrollable need. When he'd first left Reno, he'd purchased Shalimar for innumerable women, unable to make love to them unless they wore Julia's signature perfume. But it was never right. Never the perfect mixing of her own, inimitable sensual fragrance with the tenacious Oriental blend. He'd given up years ago trying to find any other woman with that unique blend of scents.

Julia felt herself succumbing to the sweet magic he'd always spun about them. She struggled to maintain her control, but discovered it had as much substance as a sand castle; tides of emotion lapped at the foundations, eroding its strength.

By her trembling, Marc knew Julia's more primitive yearnings had won out over her common sense. He took her hands in his, kissing one finger at a time, before scattering little kisses on her palm and the sensitive skin of her inner wrist. Then he brought her to her feet, pushing the crepe dress down over her hips.

As it made a shimmering black puddle on the floor,

Julia stepped out of it, standing before him, clad only in a half-slip and hose. Her hands were clasped behind her back as she studied his face. Her body was slender and firm, but it was no longer the coltish beauty of a teenager. Would he be disappointed?

"You're even more lovely than I remembered," he said, banishing her worries. "More beautiful than any man could imagine." His fingers lightly stroked her throat as his head lowered once again, the deepening kiss echoing his words.

His lips trailed sparks down her throat, along her shoulders, over the slope of her breasts, reaching their quest at her rosy nipples. First lightly, then with more strength, he took them into his mouth, each in its own turn, plucking them with his lips and tongue. When his teeth closed down to nip at one aroused, moist tip, Julia cried out and Marc licked the pain away. He was surprised to find himself shuddering with need for her.

"Undress me." His breath was a hot, desperate wind into her mouth. "Please, Julia. I want to feel you against me."

Julia's fingers were numb as they fumbled with the buttons of his shirt, but when she dared a glance up into his dark eyes, she saw only warmth and encouragement. Feeling braver, she reached out to touch his dark skin. He didn't have as much chest hair as his dark coloring would indicate, just that soft mat of curly ebony that arrowed down in an enticing funnel beyond the waistband of his slacks. She pushed the shirt off his shoulders, but her attempts to remove it entirely were halted as the sleeves remained locked onto his firm wrists.

"Cuff links," he murmured, his teeth tugging at her earlobe.

"Perhaps I should leave you like this," she suggested

with a breathless little laugh. "They're as effective as a straitjacket."

"You wouldn't do that," he groaned in agony. "Not after all the years I've dreamed of loving you again."

Love? Julia wondered how he could bandy the word around like that. She'd only ever spoken it to one man. The man whose skin was gleaming with a faint sheen of perspiration as he waited for her to undress him. God help her, she was going to do it.

The word struck a responsive chord within Marc, too, before he hastily rejected it. He wanted her—desperately—but love was for idealistic young men who'd never learned the impossibility of such a state.

"I'll release you," Julia decided, locating the square gold fasteners, "if you stop lying."

"About what?"

"You know." She lowered her head to prevent him from witnessing the warm flush darkening her cheeks. But Marc had a more vivid view as her naked skin deepened to a lustrous ruby.

"Tell me what you think I'm lying about," he coaxed. His hands were still held captive by the cuff links, but his lips brushed against her heated flesh, leaving sparks wherever they touched.

"Marc . . ."

"Tell me."

"About having dreamed of me. You don't have to say that."

"I know." His tongue trailed up her throat from her breast, flicking at her pulse spot with a treacherous touch. "I'm not lying, Julia." The use of her given name matched the sudden solemnity of his tone.

"I've dreamed of you an amazing number of times in the last fifteen years. I've never forgotten how you feel when you tremble in my arms. How you taste. The soft little sounds you make when I love you." That much at least was true.

"Liar," she whispered, freeing him finally.

Julia tilted her head invitingly for his kiss, and when he pulled her against him, she found his body was heated with the same flame that burned through her. Marc's fingers moved to her waist, massaging her skin with warming strokes. His thumbs hitched the waistbands of both slip and panty hose, peeling them down her long legs, leaving her standing before him, her soft curves gleaming in the reflected light of a harvest moon.

"Your turn," he invited, holding out his arms.

Julia felt as if she were in some type of wonderous trance, kneeling as she removed his slacks and briefs. She knew Marc heard her sharp intake of breath as she gazed up at him, so much uncompromising male.

She felt like Rip Van Winkle, her slumbering senses newly awakened by Marc's erotic caresses. But unlike that folklore character, Julia was discovering everything to be exactly the same as it had been in the past. She craved him, tonight as always; her body yearned for his touch as it had all these years. She clung to him, her fingers digging into the moist flesh of his shoulders, reeling from the impact of unadulterated desire. Beyond making any sense of this, she gave up the last vestige of control and their desperate bodies lowered to the carpet, pressed together in a need too long denied.

"I've waited for this moment for fifteen years, Juliet," he avowed huskily, planting kisses everywhere his burning eyes lingered. Marc belatedly realized bringing up the past was a fatal mistake as Julia's eyes suddenly flew open and she tensed under his touch.

"Oh, no, Please, Marc. This is all wrong."

He refused to accept the silent language of her body,

or her whispered protest as he continued covering her with a blizzard of kisses.

"No, Julia. It's not wrong at all. For once in a very long time, everything is perfect."

"Marc, you have to stop!" There was a faint edge of hysteria in her tone and Marc's hands froze on her thighs, his lips pressing against her satiny skin. For a long, silent moment he didn't move. Then slowly, reluctantly, he lifted his gaze to hers.

"Is this the way you're going to play the game? Are you back to promising things you have no intention of delivering?"

Her misty eyes begged him to accept her change of mind. "Please, Marc. I can't discuss it right now. Not like this." She could tell by the set of his jaw that Marc wasn't about to let her off easily, and she steeled herself for an argument. She felt defenseless against the passion that flowed through his veins, right along with his blood, but she was determined that he would see only a controlled, coolly competent woman now.

"You damn well can discuss it, and you will, Julia," he warned, his abrasive voice slicing through the tense air. "Because I'm not letting you go until you explain what you think you're doing. Is it your feminine ploy to hand out these little enticements, these sexual promises, holding out until you've acquired Apollo's account? Is that how you've managed to achieve such prominence in such a short professional career?"

He heard her sharp gasp and reluctantly gave her points for keeping her temper as she managed to answer in a reasonably controlled tone.

"If we do this tonight, we'll never be able to work together, Marc. The timing's all wrong." The timing was *never* right, she considered grimly. It had been wrong fifteen years ago on that moonless night when she'd given herself to him for the first time, coming alive in his arms with an explosion that had shown her, as inexperienced as she had been, the difference between sex and making love.

"Is it that you're afraid of getting pregnant?" he asked, trying to find a logical reason for her refusal. "I can take care of that, Julia. I'm certainly not without experience."

His coolly stated declaration of expertise stung her. Julia was still experiencing a lingering sexual desire, throbbing deep within her as it ebbed with excruciating slowness. Suddenly she was awash with jealousy for all the women who'd experienced the lovemaking she'd been denied all these years. She resented Marc for having abandoned her. She hated him. And she loved him. The confusion of those conflicting thoughts banished all rational behavior from her mind.

"I'll bet you're not, Marc Castellano," she retorted, glaring up at him. "But that doesn't have a damn thing to do with it!"

Marc struggled against how right she felt under his body as he worked to regain his advantage. "Ah, I was wondering how long it'd be before that famous Irish temper flared. Have you ever noticed that it's impossible for us to carry on a conversation without you resorting to yelling?"

"Perhaps that's because you're so damn—damn—" Julia struggled for a word, finding conversation difficult while she was lying on her back with Marc leaning over her so close she could feel his warm breath on her face.

"Sexy?" he supplied with a suggestive grin.

It was impossible not to feel the proof of his still-vibrant desire hard against her and she struggled to find her voice.

"No."

"Lovable?"

Damn him. Julia knew exactly why Marc was moving his hips in that blatantly seductive way. Give in, his masculine body urged. His practiced ravishment of her senses made her all too well aware of her own reescalating desire, but she successfully chilled her tone. "Certainly not."

Marc ignored her icy refusal. His lips plucked at hers, coaxing her to abandon whatever had come between them for the time being.

"Unforgettable?"

He'd hit too close to home. "Selfish," she decided, wiggling free to sit up. Drawing her knees up against her chest, she wrapped her arms around them, the rigid position designed as a shield against his probing dark eyes.

"I probably am," he agreed easily. "So are you, Julia. What's the big deal?"

"I'm not selfish, Marc. Perhaps I was when I was younger, but I'm not now. You don't know me anymore."

"That's what I was trying to do, honey," he reminded her with a wicked grin.

"Dammit, Marc, this isn't funny. We have to work together tomorrow. I don't know about you, but I take my career seriously. And I can't concentrate when I'm worried about when and where you're going to rape me."

Harsh laughter burst from his throat, and he shook his head with barely leashed anger. An icy feeling of *déjà vu* washed over Marc as her words vividly brought back her father's long-ago accusation. He rose to stand over her, his spread-legged stance meant to intimidate, but Julia secretly admitted that it was also undeniably stimulating.

"Not again! What is it with you, Julia? Is that what you honestly call what we were doing? Rape?" He gathered up his clothes from the floor, throwing them on with far more haste than Julia had discarded them. "You Cassidys must have some crazy dictionary, lady, because you wanted it every bit as much as I did."

"Of course I did." Her voice rose a full octave, "But I can't, Marc . . . not without some understanding of what's happening between us." Julia glared at him aggressively, moisture spangling her heavy lashes as angry tears spilled forth. She wiped at them with the back of her hand, sniffling inelegantly.

Marc stopped in the process of buttoning his shirt and stared at her, startled by her response. "Oh, damn," he muttered, not knowing what he'd done now but wishing all to hell he hadn't. He gathered her to him, holding her in a tight embrace, his hands moving through her tumbled waves of coppery hair. "Don't cry, Julia. You know how I hate that."

Julia's only response was to bury her head further into his shoulder. A dam seemed to have burst within her, hot tears drenching his once-crisp white shirt. Marc was stunned by her behavior and felt totally helpless as his strong hands stroked her wildly tumbled hair. He'd come here tonight wanting to see her cry. Well, he'd gotten his wish. But he didn't like it. He felt like an absolute bastard and didn't even know what he'd done to provoke this heart-wrenching reaction.

At first, this had seemed to be nothing but another one of their arguments. While he and Julia had shared a lot of love that summer, they'd also struck sparks off each other. In every way, that relationship had been a powder keg. She was right. Despite the time elapsed and the changes in both their lives, nothing seemed different.

"Hey, Irish, you're taking all this too seriously. You're not the first woman who's turned me down."

His confident air made Julia feel like an absolute idiot. What in the world must he think of her? She was acting like some hysterical, overwrought teenager and not the successful businesswoman who was attempting to win his firm's account. This was ridiculous. What was it about Marc Castellano that had her constantly spinning out of control? She pushed at his shoulders, backing away.

"You're right, of course, Marc. And I apologize. All I can say is that I've been wrapped up in my work and it's been a long time for me. And while a woman has the same needs as a man, I'm not about to sacrifice my principles just for a little sexual relief."

Julia's cool tone was like a slap in his face. Suckered again. Why the hell had he even bothered to offer solace? This woman could give Attila the Hun lessons.

Marc's eyes burned with a deadly fire. "Of course not, Julia. I would have been surprised if you had." His gaze raked over her disheveled appearance, as if he suddenly found her extremely distasteful. "So let's just forget this little reunion ever happened. You can go on with your comfortable, proper life. And I can go on with mine."

He spun on his heel, his back stiff as he moved toward her front door. Julia had seen that look once before, the day she'd left the wooded arbor with her father. Marc had hated her at that moment, just as he obviously did now. It was a shock to her entire system exactly how badly that realization hurt.

"Marc?" Her voice was soft, cautious.

"Yes?" He didn't turn around to face her.

"About the account . . ." She didn't care about the account now, but it was a link. For some unfathomable reason, she couldn't let him walk out of her life.

He slowly turned, his mouth a grim slash circled with taut white lines. "You're something else, do you know that, Julia Cassidy? A real black widow."

He saw her flinch of pain and mistakenly took it to be fear that he'd take Apollo Enterprises elsewhere. "Don't worry, sweetheart," he growled, his voice harsh, "you'll get a fair shake in the boardroom, even if you have turned out to be nothing but a tease in the bedroom. I'll listen to your pitch and give Silverado serious consideration.

"You're the perfect banker, Julia. You've got a steel-trap mind and no heart. If I needed a model for my computers, sweetheart, I sure as hell couldn't do any better than you."

He was gone before she could come up with an appropriate reply to that harsh indictment, slamming the door behind him. Julia slumped into the chair he'd vacated, deciding that this was becoming a discomforting pattern in their relationship. If Marc Castellano walked out on her one more time, she'd aim something at his perfectly shaped head.

Chapter Four

❧

In yet another display of uncharacteristic behavior, Julia arrived at her office late the next morning, only to discover that Marc had called and requested an eleven-thirty appointment.

There'd be no avoiding another meeting. She might as well get it over with as soon as possible, she thought, although after last night she wouldn't be at all surprised if Marc was going to tell her Silverado was the last bank in the world he wanted to do business with. It would be just like him to deliver the bad news in person.

"Call Mr. Castellano back and tell him that's fine," Julia instructed Marge, glancing at her open appointment book with a sigh.

She had the owner of several grain elevators in the Midwest scheduled for that hour, but she'd worked with Jim Bannister long enough to know he'd jump at an excuse to remain in Reno another day. She'd seen him last night, coming out of Harrah's with a gorgeous showgirl on each arm. No, he wouldn't object in the slightest to her rescheduling their appointment.

Your meeting with Marc won't take all day, an errant little voice in the back of her mind reminded her. You can schedule Bannister for later in the afternoon.

"Shut up," she muttered.

"What did you say?" Marge pushed in the doorway to Julia's office, her blue eyes widening.

Julia shook her head, laughing a tense, artificial laugh. Now she was talking to herself. No doubt about it, she was definitely going bonkers.

"Nothing. I was just mumbling about life in general."

"Well, speaking about life in particular, I wouldn't mind Silverado getting Marc Castellano's account. That's a waste, don't you think?"

"A waste?"

"Yeah. A gorgeous hunk like that wasting his life on machines."

"I'm sure he doesn't spend all his time on computers," Julia said dryly, recalling his statement about all those other women.

"That's what I'm counting on." Marge grinned before returning to her desk in the outer office. Julia watched her, realizing the woman's dress was new and a far cry from those her secretary usually wore in order to maintain the almost stuffy atmosphere of Silverado Fidelity Bank.

Bracing her elbows on her desktop, Julia cupped her chin in her palms and stared absently out the window at the mirrored tower. Why in the world was she even trying to bridge the gap between them? Marc obviously had women falling at his feet. He didn't even like her. Oh, she knew he wanted her, but lust was an easily satiated sensation. Once he got what he wanted, he'd move on to other women. He'd certainly proven that before, and from his words last night, he hadn't changed.

Later that morning Marc stood in the doorway of Julia's office, watching her arguing with her desktop computer. All it took was one look and any remaining anger of the previous night disintegrated like fog under a blazing sun. She was so lovely. Lovelier than ever, although he had to stifle his laughter as he realized Julia had indeed grown up. At seventeen, she hadn't even known some of the words she was muttering now.

"What is it now, Marge?" Julia's eyes flashed as she looked up from the computer screen, catching a movement in the doorway.

"That's what I love to see, a woman enjoying her work."

His deep voice was laced with amusement and Julia glared at him. She was too absorbed in her own exacerbation to harbor any embarrassment over the fiasco of last night.

"Don't you dare laugh at me, Marc Castellano. I'm close to violence and I may decide it's less expensive to throw something at you than through this damn screen."

"May I offer some assistance?" He remained where he was, his long legs crossed as he leaned against the door frame.

"I know I copied my file on Hudson oil, but this . . . this *monster* won't admit he's hiding it! He keeps repeating 'illegal command.' Which is a ridiculous term, when you think about it. Is someone going to burst in from IBM and arrest me for trying to retrieve a file?"

"You're probably not asking politely enough. Do you always refer to your office help as monsters?"

"This help"—Julia jerked her auburn head in the direction of the screen with its blinking fluorescent green message—"creates as many problems as it solves. We haven't seen byte to eyeball since he arrived."

"You're allowing it to intimidate you, Julia. It's just a machine."

"Sure. A machine who gleefully rubs his little cables together whenever he sees me coming. 'How are we going to drive Julia Cassidy crazy today?' he cackles, grinding his disk drives." Her eyes were wide and distressful as she watched Marc move across the room. "I know it, Marc. He's out to get me."

"What file do you want?"

Marc leaned over her shoulder, his long dark fingers poised over the computer keyboard, and Julia fought against the flood of sensations caused by his nearness. Everything about him conspired to drive business from her mind. The crisp tang of his after-shave was more pungent than an autumn bonfire, and his breath was a warm breeze, stirring her hair. She could feel the heat radiating from his body, and her fingertips tingled with tactile memory of his warm, hard chest.

"What?" She stared up into the dark face directly above her, his question driven from her mind by her sensual musings.

"The file?"

"Oh, Hudson Oil . . . but it's gone, Marc. This dreadful machine ate it. I know it did. I promised to have the information on George's desk by this afternoon, and it's gone."

"Hudson Oil," he murmured, his fingers tapping the keys.

From the trail of false commands still printed on the screen, Marc recognized Julia's dilemma as an easy problem to solve. A high-school computer buff could do it in two seconds flat. But it took all of his concentration as the scent of Shalimar rose from her velvety soft skin.

From this vantage point, he had an enticing view of her breasts as they swelled against her silk blouse. His body stirred rebelliously as he remembered the taste and feel of her, and his fingers itched, as if they'd much rather be busy with the ascot tie at the blouse's neck than this keyboard.

"There you go," he stated as the screen filled with columns of numbers. "Hudson Oil. Right where you left it."

Julia's smile was radiant, her eyes lit with gratitude. "Thank you, Marc. You've just saved my job."

Mark felt a stab of disloyalty when he remembered how often he'd fantasized costing Julia her position at Silverado Fidelity.

"You just need to develop more patience, Julia. As I recall, it never was one of your more dominant traits."

She jerked her eyes away from his devilish gaze, focusing on the data on the screen in front of her. "How did you know how to do that?"

He shrugged. "It's a fairly simple program. In fact, it's one I played with for a time over at IBM before I left to establish Apollo."

"Oh." That made sense. At any rate, the important thing was that she'd be able to print it up in time for George's conference with Matthew Hudson. She excused herself, promising Marc they'd discuss his account as soon as she instructed Marge to activate the printer they shared.

"This is ridiculous." Julia expelled an exasperated breath when she and Marc were interrupted again.

For the past thirty minutes they'd been trying to conduct a business conversation, but it seemed as if every female in the bank had come up with an emergency only Julia could solve. Like contestants in a beauty contest, they'd trooped in and out of her office in a steady parade.

"You seem to be very important around here," Marc commented, his dark eyes dancing as he invited her to join in the humor of their situation.

Julia failed to return his smile. She had no doubt Marc was used to such things. The man was like the Pied Piper, although in this case *he* was the rat.

"Well, we're certainly not going to get anything accomplished this way," she stated briskly. "How do you feel about lunch?"

"Sounds great," he agreed. "You buying?"

"Of course, isn't that how it's done?" She smiled finally, a genuine, teasing grin. "Remember, Marc, in this courtship I'm the wooer, you're the wooee."

"Woo away, Juliet, I'm all yours."

His voice was like a velvet embrace; Julia was shaken, but not surprised by the instant flash of heat that arced between them. They'd always affected each other like a jolt of lightning, but he always left her hurting.

Julia had responded to Marc's vibrant masculinity the first time she'd seen him making a delivery of wine to the country club. His dark hair had gleamed in the sun and his muscles had rippled below the sleeves he'd rolled up to the elbow as he loaded the wooden crates from the truck labeled Castellano Distributing.

Jerking upright on her lounge chair, Julia shook the young woman next to her, who lay dozing in the summer sun. "Meredith, do you know who that is?"

Her friend mumbled an inarticulate reply, refusing to rouse from her blissful relaxation.

Julia still hadn't taken her eyes off the breathtakingly handsome young man, following his every lithe movement as she jabbed her friend in the bare ribs.

"Meredith, I want to know who he is."

Exhaling a sigh of sheer exasperation, Meredith Janzen lifted herself up onto her elbows, blinking blindly in the sunlight for a moment. Then, following Julia's enraptured gaze, she nodded her sleek blond head in understanding.

"No wonder you woke me up. That's Marc Castellano."

"Why haven't I ever seen him before?"

Julia knew she was staring, but she couldn't take her eyes off him. He was so beautiful. An odd word to use for a man, but it fit Marc Castellano perfectly. Tall and whip-cord lean, he moved with a loose-limbed stride that was pantherlike in its grace. Julia could tell that his body, under the denim shirt and jeans, was hard and firm.

When he bent down to pick up a crate of Pinot Noir, his shirt pulled loose from his waistband, exposing enough of his dark back to display the rippling of long, corded muscles. Julia experienced a shock low in her body and wondered at the unusual warmth it inspired.

"He's been away at Cal Poly for the past four years. And before that he only spent summers in Reno. He went to boarding school, military school, something like that," Meredith explained, her amused gaze moving from the man to her friend.

"Besides," she continued, "our families don't really move in the same circles as the Castellanos. Can you imagine sitting down to a white-tie dinner with a bunch of gamblers and the type of people who probably hang around that casino?"

"Is he a gambler, do you think?" Julia asked, her avid gaze on his back, wishing he'd turn around so she could see his face again. She concentrated, as if she could send the message by telepathy.

"Probably." Meredith shrugged, lying back on her lounge with the supple grace of a spoiled kitten. "Look all you want, Julia, but the guy's off limits, even if you could pique his interest. From the gossip, though, I'd say you're not his type. He's been dating showgirls from the Castellano casino since he was sixteen."

Just then, Julia's intense mental effort was rewarded as Marc Castellano turned. His eyes met hers directly in an intense, knowing gaze and a thousand messages flashed between them in a span of seconds, every one more provocative than the last. Julia felt like she was sinking rapidly into quicksand. His eyes burned through the heavy lenses of her prescription sunglasses, like jet lasers, and she could feel her blood thicken and heat in response. Her heart lurched wildly as he broke the gaze, a blistering scowl on his face as he returned to work.

Meredith lifted her sunglasses to the top of her blond head. "Close your mouth, Julia, you look like a grounded trout."

"Julia?" Marc's deep voice sliced through her reverie, bringing her back to reality.

"I'm sorry, Marc. I was deciding where to eat lunch."

"From the expression on your face, I'll accept."

"What?"

"I've had plenty of breakfasts in bed in my day, but a lunch in bed will be a nice change. I like a bank with such a personal touch, Juliet."

"I don't know what you're talking about. I wasn't thinking anything of the kind."

"Sure," he agreed, far too quickly for comfort. Her instincts were proven right when he attacked from a new direction. "By the way, whatever happened to that friend of yours? Meredith Janzen?"

"How did you know—" Julia bit off the question, almost severing her tongue as her teeth crashed together.

"You were wearing a strawberry-pink bikini, which should have clashed with all that red hair, but for some reason didn't. Your slim young body was glistening with coconut oil and you had little beads of moisture between your breasts. You looked good enough to eat, sweetheart." His eyes softened as they made a leisurely tour of the portion of her body in view above the top of the desk. "You still do, as a matter of fact. Why don't we forgo lunch and start with dessert?"

Julia reached for the telephone, utilizing every ounce of her willpower to keep her hands from shaking. "I'm getting us a table for lunch. And to keep these little misunderstandings from arising again, I don't know what got into me last night. It was probably a response from overwork, too much champagne at dinner, and too many old memories. I want your account, Marc, but I won't go to bed with you to get it."

"I never thought you would, Julia," Marc returned blandly, seeming unperturbed by her cool declaration.

"I'm glad we have that settled," she murmured, her fingernails pushing the Lucite buttons with renewed strength.

"When you go to bed with me, it will be because you want it as badly as I do, sweetheart. We both know business will be the farthest thing from your mind."

Marc kept the conversation impersonal as Julia drove them to the restaurant. He arched a brow as she led him to the compact Dodge Colt, but he made no comment. Inwardly he was surprised she'd chosen such a practical, spartan vehicle. He wondered idly what had happened to that Corvette convertible she'd driven past Castellano Distributors time after time that summer.

She'd been an irrepressible vixen, her sex appeal and feminine self-confidence more than any seventeen-year-old should have been gifted with. He'd done everything humanly possible to avoid her seductive lairs, spotting them with the ease a wary fox sights a snare in the forest. She'd collected male scalps for amusement, and it still rankled that his had joined the ranks of all those inexperienced teenage boys.

He kept the conversation on neutral ground, commenting on the crisp tang of the autumn weather, the changes in Reno during the fifteen years of his absence, and the development that had sprung up around the lake. While grateful for his behavior, Julia knew neither of them was fooled. The electricity sparked about them in the close interior of her car.

"Victoria's," he murmured as she pulled into the parking lot of the restaurant. "Do they still make that terrific crab quiche?"

Julia laughed, slanting him a teasing glance. "I thought real men didn't eat quiche, Marc."

He reached out, brushing his knuckles along her cheekbone, feeling her shiver in response. "If you've got any doubts along those lines, Juliet, I'll be glad to put your fears to rest."

Oh, God, she agonized, why was it so easy for him? How was it that he could affect her with the slightest touch, the simplest statement, the most casual look? She was used to exchanging light banter with men; that had been the reason for the teasing quip about the quiche. But with Marc there were no innocent conversations, no impersonal touches. He had branded her his own in the most elemental way a long time ago and she'd never responded like this to any other man.

"Don't bother, Marc. I'm more than willing to take your word for it."

"That's not very scientific."

"I'm a banker, not a scientist."

"Ah, but I am, Julia. And you must admit, in order to figure out how to get my account, you need to understand how I think. Don't they refer to it as pushing the right buttons?"

Julia crossed her arms over her chest, eyeing him cautiously. "To a point, although it's not as calculating as you make it sound."

"I'm sure you don't have a calculating bone in that lovely body," Marc replied dryly, his expression belying his words. "However, you should realize that I always utilize the scientific method to keep my life functioning in an orderly fashion."

"I see," she said briskly, showing little interest as she reached for the keys in the ignition.

Marc caught her hand, his fingers entwining with hers as his thumb rubbed little circles on the tender skin of her palm. "Sit still, Ms. Cassidy, and I'll give the lady banker the secret to my success."

"I suppose I'm going to get it whether I want it or not," she retorted.

"Of course. Now, first we state the problem. Let's see, how do we put it delicately? I wonder how it would be to make love to the delectable Julia Cassidy after all these years."

"Marc, please—"

He pressed a finger against her lips, cutting off her soft protest. "Hush, you're getting a free science lesson. Now, on to formulating the hypothesis . . . I consider what I already know of the problem: that the very sight of you stirs my blood, that your scent intoxicates me in the way no alcohol has ever done and the touch of your hand anywhere on my body turns my skin to flame. And, most important, past experience tells me that no one has ever topped you, Julia. No one."

Marc's pupils flared with a definite hunger as he held her gaze. Julia felt her body trembling and knew she was handing him more facts for his outrageous hypothesis.

"Next step," he murmured, releasing her hand. He unbuttoned her cashmere coat before running his fingers along the ridge of her collarbone. "Observance and experimentation . . . Your body trembles when I touch you here."

His roving hand feathered enticingly at the base of her throat, feeling the response of her blood as it leapt to his touch.

"And here." Marc did not miss Julia's quick intake of breath as his fingers traveled slowly downward. "And here."

Julia shook her head in a slow, negative motion, unable to move away from the increasing intimacy of his touches. He'd only brushed his treacherous fingers along the slope of her breasts, but she could feel her nipples gathering themselves into expectant little points, and risked a glance downward.

"See? A very good sign." His gaze moved with hers to the pebbled crowns pushing at the dark-russet silk of her blouse. "Observation points to the conclusion that our experiments will be quite successful, Julia. But to be positive, we'll need repeated experimentation. Are you sure you don't want to pass on this lunch?"

His dark gaze was compelling, enticing her into complacency with every atom of sexuality Marc possessed. Julia fought against it, knowing that, were she to give in now, when he was so blatantly insisting upon her capitulation, she'd never survive.

She assumed an attitude of casual nonchalance. "You're using inductive reasoning, Marc, when I'm willing to settle for deductive. I have enough knowlege of past events to enable me to draw my own conclusion. And I'm not nearly as optimistic as you." She turned away, preparing to exit the car.

"Ah, but you're forgetting one important scientific principle, love," he stated calmly.

She eyed him warily over her shoulder. "And what's that?"

"The accuracy of deductive logic depends on the accuracy of the principles and rules used. I'd say your data is weak if you're basing it all on that disastrous last time fifteen years ago."

Julia remembered Marc standing up to her father, all

steely strength and purpose, insisting that he loved her and that she loved him. He had remained incredibly forceful for someone without a stitch of clothing on, she considered, even to this day giving him credit for an unshakable presence.

James Cassidy had remained unruffled in the face of such furious emotion. He'd simply ignored Marc's outburst and asked Julia, with cool disregard for her own disheveled appearance, if she was ready to come home with him. It had been Julia's intention to talk it out with her parents, explain that she and Marc were right for each other, and ask their blessing.

When approval wasn't forthcoming, Julia returned to the secret, wooded spot at Lake Tahoe, but Marc hadn't been there. After a long, lonely night spent huddling against the cold, terrified by the sounds of woodland animals scurrying about in the shadows, she accepted the truth. She'd been a summer dalliance for a man who'd always intended to leave Reno—and her—all along.

Forcing the painful memory from her mind, Julia scrambled from the car. She was standing in the parking lot, searching for an appropriate answer to Marc's accusation when the strident sound of an alarm shattered her concentration.

"What in the world?" She was nearly in tears as she stared down at her car.

"Your keys." The corner of Marc's mouth quirked. "You left them in the ignition."

"I was going to take them out," Julia insisted, yanking them from the steering column. "I hadn't forgotten them."

"I never said you had, Irish." Marc laughed, his hand resting possessively on her back as he walked with her up to the restaurant door.

Victoria's was a rambling, two-story house that had

been a popular bordello in Nevada's frontier days. Maintaining the old-time western decor, it had been completely remodeled, and the small bedrooms upstairs were now private dining rooms. It was to one of these that the hostess led Julia and Marc.

"I won't say another word if you want to order the quiche, Marc," Julia said lightly, smiling at him over the top of the leather-bound menu.

His only response was a muffled grunt as he kept his eyes glued to the list.

Now what had she done? "Marc? Is something wrong?"

He shook his head, mumbling a negative. Then he suddenly slammed the menu down with enough force to rattle the tall water goblets.

"Yes, dammit, there *is* something wrong. And if you can't understand it, you're as shallow and shortsighted as you ever were."

His words were forced out between tightly clenched teeth and Julia was shocked at the matching acerbity in his eyes. She stared at him in confusion.

"Then I guess I'm shallow. I haven't the faintest idea what you're upset about."

"It's this place." He waved his hand around the room.

Julia's brow furrowed as her eyes narrowed behind her glasses. "Victoria's? But you said you liked it here. We can go somewhere else, Marc, that's no problem."

She half-rose from the table, but he reached out and grasped her arm, pushing her back to the burgundy velvet chair.

"Victoria's is fine," Marc's replied, watching her closely, "but what would you say if I insisted we eat downstairs?"

"Downstairs? In the main dining room?"

"Smart lady. No wonder Stevenson gave you your own

office. You must stun them daily with your mental calisthenics."

"Knock it off, Marc," Julia flung back, irritation finally replacing distress at his behavior. "If you want to eat downstairs, it's fine with me. But the place is a madhouse at noon. I didn't think we could get any more work done down there than we could in my office. But I'm willing to try."

Julia's pointed gaze moved to his strong hand still covering her sleeve. "If you'll take your hand off me, then I won't have to walk past everyone looking as if I'm being held hostage."

His expression remained grim, but she saw a shadow of doubt gather in his dark eyes. "That's all it was? You didn't want to be bothered by the noise?"

Julia expelled an exasperated breath, taking a long drink of ice water with her free hand. "Of course. What did you think it was? That I wanted you alone to seduce you? You've got a funny way of handling that, Marc."

Marc didn't release her, but his fingers loosened considerably. "No. I thought you were still ashamed to be seen in public with me."

His voice was sharp, but Julia saw a fleeting vulnerability in his eyes and could have wept. She slowly put her glass down, covering his hand with hers. "Marc, please believe me, that idea never entered my mind."

His dark gaze speared her intently as he searched for the truth in her softened features. How could he trust her? His advantage in age and experience was certainly no protection. He'd been four years older and worlds more experienced than Julia Cassidy fifteen years ago. And look where that had gotten him.

"If that's true," he said finally, "prove it."

"How can I do that?"

"Come out with me tonight. Dinner, a show, the works. Wherever I want to go."

"Marc—"

He cut her off, his free hand slicing through the air. "It's important to you in more ways than one, Julia. Because I won't put my money in any institution that's ashamed to have me bring it through the front door."

There was such a wealth of bitterness in his tone that Julia gasped. "You've got everything all wrong," she protested.

She tried to think of something, anything, to prove that she was not ashamed of him—that she'd never been ashamed of him. She had always thought Marc understood her behavior that long-ago summer, that meeting him secretly was the only way she could see him. Still a minor, her parents' threats had been clear, her choices few. Had he mistakenly taken her behavior for class snobbery? Stunned by that revelation, Julia's anger dissolved like sugar crystals in hot tea.

"I'll go out with you on two conditions," she agreed.

His black brows rose in speculation. "And they are?"

"First, that you agree to discuss business with me during lunch—not your scientific curiosity about our sexual compatibility, nor anything about the past—business. Banking and high-tech."

"That's easy. I can agree to that," Marc stated, relaxing his hold on her arm even further. "What's the second?"

"That you don't spend this evening trying to seduce me. I'm really not up to fighting you all night."

He shook his head, his eyes remaining on her face. "That's just the point, Julia. I don't want to fight with you all night. I want to love you all night."

"No."

"Fine." He released her arm and slid his hand out from under hers. "Thanks for the lunch offer, but suddenly I'm not very hungry. Besides, I need to find another bank before I transfer Apollo's home office here." He rose abruptly from the table.

She stared up at him. "That's ridiculous. You won't find a bank anywhere in the state capable of handling your business as well as Silverado. I can't believe you're willing to settle for less simply because I won't go to bed with you."

Marc shoved his hands into his pockets, rocking back and forth on his heels as he gave her a long, level gaze. "You've got it all wrong, Julia. I'm settling for a different bank because you're stating categorically that you won't give me a chance. I'm supposed to give you a chance to prove your offer is right for me, but you won't allow me the same privilege."

Julia stirred uneasily in her chair. Her eyes escaped his chiding gaze long enough for her to light a much-needed cigarette. When she reluctantly, warily, lifted her eyes back to the silent man standing over her, she shook her head in bewilderment.

"You're kidding. Marc, you can't compare banking and lovemaking in one breath. That's no way to do business."

Marc's expression assured he wasn't joking. "I've been accused of being too emotional before, Julia. Because I make gut decisions that have paid off for me so far. I'm working now in a field others consider nothing but pure bunk because I've got this crazy feeling it's going to be bigger than anything since Edison invented the electric light bulb."

He folded his arms across his chest, his stance one of implacable purpose. "I'm just as positive I don't want to do business with a bank that only sees me as figures on its ledger sheet. I want a more personal relationship than that."

Julia's auburn eyebrows flew above the tortoiseshell

frame of her glasses. "Are you telling me you'll only put your money where the banker will sleep with you?"

A little smile played over Marc's full lips as he thought of most of the bankers he knew. No, he definitely had not felt a need to sleep with them.

"Of course not. But I'm only willing to put my money into your bank if you drop that ridiculous restriction. I'm not saying you *have* to sleep with me, Julia. I just want you to give me a chance to prove it's right—for both of us."

"I don't know which of us is crazier, Marc," she sighed, shaking her head as she picked up her menu once again. "But sit down, you've got yourself a deal. And a date."

He gave her a rakish grin. "I'm glad you see it my way, Julia. I would have been extremely disappointed if I had to walk out just now."

Julia watched him cautiously. "Oh?"

The smile he gave her was boyishly charming. "Of course. My car is at your office and that's a hell of a long walk. Besides, my mouth has been watering for Victoria's crab quiche since you pulled into the parking lot."

Julia stuck her tongue out at him, shocking herself by her response. She was further humiliated when she realized the waitress had arrived at that moment, catching her childish behavior. Marc was no help. He roared with laughter, his head thrown back, delighting in her discomfort.

Chapter Five

"Now it's your turn to tell me about your work," Julia requested as they ate the superbly prepared lunch.

Marc, true to his word, had ordered the crab quiche, and Julia carefully avoided opening up that suggestive topic. She had spent the time selling the benefits of Silverado and felt it was now time to let him talk about his own work. She'd learned long ago that men tended to resent women who appeared too forthright in the banking field, and it was a delicate tightrope she maneuvered—that of being assertive and purposeful without crossing over to aggressive and pushy.

"It's incredibly exciting." Marc put down his fork, directing his full attention to his answer. She tried not to be affected by the way his face lit with boyish enthusiasm.

"We're standing on the threshold of a new frontier and there are no limits to what we can achieve."

"It's bad enough watching people be replaced by automatic tellers." She laughed. "I'm not certain I'm ready to be replaced by a robot."

"Ah, that's where the distinction lies." Marc pushed his plate aside, resting his elbows on the table as he made a tent with his fingers. "Robots have a lot of brawn and not much brain. What we're talking about here is a machine with a mind of its own."

"That's impossible," she stated. "Isn't it?"

"Not at all. There's already something called an androbot on the market. He's a combination robot and android who's proving it's possible to build an artificial intelligence machine. He's still very young, but believe me, his growth is going to be at a far greater pace than a human's. The knowledge is growing exponentially, Julia. It's incredible."

"Frightening, you mean," she said. "I saw the movie *2001*, Marc. What happens if you get a paranoid computer like HAL?"

"There's another side to that which the Defense Department has already considered," he argued, nodding at the waitress who'd arrived to take their plates. "Would you like some coffee? Or do you have to get back to the office?"

Julia silently blessed Jim Bannister's instant acquiescence in moving his appointment to the next day. "I'd love coffee, and I'm in no hurry."

"You have to realize that a computer isn't just another machine, like a dishwasher or an airplane. It's an information-processing machine, which is, in part, what we are. Think of it, Julia—ours is the first age to witness a face-to-face encounter of natural and artificial intelligence."

Julia watched the glow of enthusiasm warm his face and brighten his eyes. Marc had looked that way at her once upon a time, in a world she'd put far, far behind her. Her mouth pressed into a tight line, her teeth chewing irritably at her bottom lip. Then it struck her. She was jealous . . . of a computer! Julia Cassidy, MBA, hotshot investment banker, was making mincemeant of her lips because Marc Castellano obviously adored his work more than her.

Lost in his explanation, Marc failed to note the staggering truth as it marched uncensored across Julia's face. He continued thoughtfully, his dark gaze focused on something far beyond this private dining room in an old boom-town bordello.

"It's thrilling, but, admittedly, a bit frightening. Right now we're headed down dark passages, finding our way a step at a time. It's bound to change how we think about ourselves."

He stopped to take a sip of his coffee. "Good," he announced. "A nice mellow blend of Colombian, Mexican, and . . ." He took another sip, furrowing his brow thoughtfully. "Santos, I think. But I like yours better."

Julia laughed. "Do you know, you're the only person I've ever met who can actually tell the difference in coffee? I know a few tea nuts, but you're the only man I know who doesn't just settle for mountain-grown without knowing which mountain it's been grown on."

Marc shrugged. "Everyone needs at least one idiosyncrasy, don't you think? Otherwise we wouldn't stand out from the crowd. I'd like to point out my coffee drinking managed to lodge in your mind well enough. And we all know how miserable you are at remembering personal things."

Julia looked down into her own cup, unwilling to meet his teasing gaze. It wasn't just the coffee, she could have argued. Everything about Marc Castellano had been indelibly inscribed onto her mind, seared there by the passion.

"You were telling me about the Defense Department," she reminded him softly.

"That's right. We agreed to nothing personal until tonight, didn't we?"

Julia didn't dare meet his eyes; she knew they would be echoing the laughter in his voice and was relieved when he kept his word.

"DARPA, the Pentagon's Defense Advanced Research Projects Agency, more than any other group, is responsible for the shape of computer science today. The first supercomputer was a DARPA project, as was time-sharing. Computer graphics, used now for everything from desktop computers to video arcade games, to those in F-16 cockpits, came from DARPA projects."

She remembered his reluctance to discuss his EFT encrypting work and probed delicately. "Are you able to tell me what you're working on, or is it top secret?"

"The grant, as well as basic facts about the Strategic Computer and Survivability project, is a matter of public record, so I can give you the gist of our work. The project's goal is to develop a variety of new machines.

"Our portion of the work is a study for the Pentagon of the mechanisms that must exist for people to reason. That way we can endow reasoning skills through an approach that permits computers to manage a wider range of information."

"You're doing this for the Pentagon? Why?"

"They feel that the smart computer could be extremely useful in war or nuclear crisis, because of its ability to keep a cool head."

The thought of computers influencing such things was not a pleasant one. Wouldn't it make war that much easier? she wondered. Not wanting to argue, she asked simply, "What do you think about that?"

Marc shrugged, running his finger along the edge of his cup. "I don't honestly know. I can see the appeal to the military. Those guys have always been into gadgetry, and the idea of drone aircraft, unmanned submarines, and land vehicles that could be sent off to do high-risk jobs is right up their alley."

He grinned. "It'd be a lot like playing an arcade war game; imagine all the nifty little things you could send off on missions around the world."

While Julia didn't want to trigger yet another disagreement, she couldn't ignore the apprehension such an idea triggered. "I'm not sure I like the idea of generals playing games with my world, Marc. It sounds as if those guys might start a war just so they could play with their high-tech toys."

He gave his head a quick, negative shake. "Let's face it, Julia, weapons have been improving since the first time a guy thought to tie a rock onto a stick. Computers aren't going to change human nature."

At her doubtful expression, Marc continued. "Besides, you don't need to worry about that scenario yet. An intelligent missile-guidance system is definitely not right around the corner. We have to bring together all the different technologies: real-time signal processing, numerical calculations, and symbolic processing. And we have to do that at unimaginably high speeds for the computer to make decisions and give advice to humans.

"Right now artificial-intelligence research is only a small tributary flowing into the mainstream of computer knowledge. Building intelligence into a machine is not like building a computer. No matter how quick and clever computers become, they're still apathetic. They couldn't care less what's happening out there. All that matters is what you feed into them."

Intrigued by his fervent defense of his work, Julia gazed at him with admiration. Suddenly their eyes met and they both stared a moment too long. Marc broke the extended gaze first, lifting the cup of lukewarm coffee to his lips. It could have been an instant brew for all he noticed, his whirling mind was so overcome with desire for Julia Cassidy.

"Where was I? That's right, smart computers . . . To create intelligence, you have to build in something that's still a mystery in humans. Curiosity. Outside a very narrow range of subjects it'll be years before we've developed a machine with reasoning ability. Hopefully, by then, we'll have achieved the ability to use it wisely."

"Don't you ever feel like Dr. Frankenstein?" she asked, her smile only partially masking the seriousness of her query.

"Always," he stated, not making light of her question. "Believe me, Julia, I'm doing my best to see that my monster doesn't run amuck. Everyone else I know in artificial-intelligence research feels the same way. We're not out to create some type of unfeeling master race with steel-trap minds and no hearts."

His words were the same ones he'd flung at her last night, and by her sharp intake of breath Marc realized what he'd done. For some reason he wanted to erase that pain from her suddenly pale, but very beautiful face.

She'd been enticing at seventeen, possessing a wild, coltish beauty, but now . . . now her haunting loveliness almost took his breath away. The distress on her face was at odds with the perfect symmetry of her features and Marc wondered at her apparent vulnerability. Julia Cassidy was a puzzle wrapped in an enigma—the most compelling woman he'd ever encountered. She had matured into a far more intelligent and complex woman than he'd imagined. He'd have to be careful if he wanted to achieve his long-awaited revenge. At this moment, he wasn't sure he still wanted it. It was not in Marc Castellano's nature to vacillate, and he turned his mind away from that problem, returning to the more immediate one of coaxing a smile back onto her voluptuous, sweet lips.

"Hey, I didn't mean that, you know." He pried her fingers from around her cup, lacing them with his longer, darker ones on the tablecloth. "You frustrated me, Julia, and I said some things I shouldn't have. I'm beginning to realize that while you're every bit as delectable as you were at seventeen, you've grown up considerably. Will you accept my apology?"

"Not only will I accept it, Marc," Julia said with a shaky laugh. "I think I'll have it bronzed, since it's the first one I've ever heard you offer."

He laughed with her, a rich, deep sound. "You've just forgotten the others."

"No way, Marc Castellano. That's something even my brain couldn't misplace."

Julia finally acknowledged they'd lingered over the refilled coffeecups long enough. Too long, she admitted honestly. There was no longer any reason to prolong their discussion. She'd brought along the pertinent information for him to study; all that remained now was for Marc to take the data home and make his decision.

About that, she was of two minds. If he chose Silverado, she'd be in close contact with him, since his electronics firm would represent one of her major accounts. There were aspects of that on both sides of the ledger sheet, and for every positive point, there was one equally negative.

If he chose another bank, she'd honestly have no excuse to keep seeing him. That thought upset her even more than the first. Her personal life had never before interfered with her business, yet Julia could not honestly decide what she wanted his decision to be.

Marc accepted the material across the table, resolving to read it that afternoon and make his damn decision.

The entire matter was becoming far more complicated than he'd planned. Initially, he'd only pretended interest in her bank because he knew Apollo would represent a major plum of an account. If Julia was as self-serving as he remembered, she'd be willing to do anything to get it, even making love to him—having sex with him, he corrected firmly.

Marc had believed that was all she was capable of; love required too much sacrifice, something Julia Cassidy would be incapable of. He'd planned to use her, discard her, and driving in the final thrust, take his business elsewhere. That was the master plan, as carefully constructed as anything a computer could devise.

But he'd left out the possibility of emotional involvement. That nagging little variable was threatening to invalidate his carefully conceived equation. Marc had created Apollo Enterprises by relying on deep-seated instincts. And that intuition was telling him that he might have misjudged Julia.

Oh, not what she had been at seventeen. Her father's little visit with the sheriff had shown exactly what she'd thought of their relationship. No, she'd been nothing but a spoiled brat in those days, only interested in the thrill of sampling forbidden fruits.

But now. He'd heard her brittle defense of him during that conversation with that imbecile Charles Stevenson. She'd had no way of knowing he was listening; it couldn't have been an act. Even if all she was after this time was his business, it wouldn't have been necessary to defend a potential client that way.

To top the whole damn thing off, Marc considered, hating his atypical indecision, the banking package she was offering was honestly the best he'd seen. But even if he abandoned his long-awaited revenge, how could he do business with her on a daily basis?

What a goddamn mess. Since when had he let his personal life interfere with his business life? Since he'd let Julia Cassidy back into his heart, Marc glumly answered his own question as they left the restaurant.

"Thank you for lunch."

Marc was not in any hurry to leave the intimate confines of her car. Even now the scent of Shalimar was like an enticing mist and he wanted to bury his lips in that soft hollow at the base of her throat.

"It was my pleasure," Julia replied blithely, smiling a bright, professional smile. "It's not often that I have the opportunity to squire around a handsome, successful man."

"That's probably because they're all too busy courting the lovely woman behind the banker."

The provocative gleam in Marc's dark eyes threatened to be her undoing as Julia struggled against the sensuality it invoked.

She turned away, her hand on the car door handle. "Not really, Marc. I'm too busy for much of a social life."

"Wait."

The request was softly issued, but held the power to hypnotize her. Julia turned slowly back to him, once again experiencing the sensation of sinking into quicksand as their gazes met.

"I have work to do, Marc."

His eyes didn't leave hers. "So do I. It's not easy moving a multimillion-dollar operation. Especially for a guy who lives in the same apartment he moved into ten years ago because it's too much of a pain to pack everything into boxes and cart it across town.

"I kept my promise during lunch," he reminded her, reaching out to absently twist a long tendril of auburn hair around his finger. The curls had escaped their tight confinement once again, framing her face in soft clouds of sunlit mahogany.

"You did," she agreed. "And I appreciate it. It's hard to keep my mind on business." She smiled a crooked smile of admittance. "Other things keep interfering."

His eyes took on a strange expression, the silent appraisal extending for what seemed an eternity. Marc finally broke the prolonged silence.

"I can't get over how honest you are these days, Julia. It's a little unsettling. Especially when you seem so determined to deny us what we both want. And need." He spoke with a roughness he made no attempt to conceal.

"I've always been honest with you, Marc," she protested in a soft whisper, turning her head to brush her lips against the fingers playing in her hair.

"Don't, Julia. God, please don't blow it with that damn lie." Marc muttered the enigmatic remark on a harsh sigh.

"What are you talking about? I haven't lied to you."

"What the hell," he muttered, a humorless line of resignation to his features as he reached out and took off her glasses, placing them on the dashboard. His eyes glittered to life as they moved restlessly over her face, the hungry black gaze vivid against clear whites.

Marc's mouth covered hers, trapping Julia's protest in her throat. He claimed her lips with a hunger he'd managed to restrain all during their business luncheon, parting her tender lips with an insistent pressure.

His tongue was a surging brand, brushing flames into all the hollowed recesses of the dark cavern of her mouth. It probed and nudged and coaxed her own into a sensual mating duel until Julia's passion flared as high and as volcanic as Marc's.

He buried his hands in the tangled thickness of her

hair, holding her to his drugging warmth. Julia welcomed the deep possession of his kiss, her own lips hungry in their need. Her determination to resist his seduction faltered; at this brilliant moment she could not think past the splendor of losing herself in the glory of his arms once again.

His hand slid under her hair, holding the back of her neck as he tilted her auburn head, dragging his mouth from the pliant warmth of her lips.

His kisses scorched her skin as he moved down the slender column of her throat, plucking at the delicate cord as his lips burrowed below the neckline of her silk blouse where he felt the wild fluttering of her pulse.

The blouse was not designed for lovemaking, the ascot tie held firmly in place by a topaz stickpin and the dark silk fastened by fabric-covered buttons down the back. But that failed to stop Marc. His lips roamed down the slope of her breasts, his breath warming her skin through the material until her nipples thrust against the heated silk in desperate need for his touch.

Julia gasped as an inexplicable pleasure rippled through her. She reached out, moving her hands down the smooth, taut planes of his chest, where she could feel the heat radiating from his body. He was on fire. Oh, Lord, had she done that to his body? Was is possible that she could still bring him to such levels of arousal?

"Oh, Juliet, see what we could have had instead of that crab quiche?" He groaned, his husky rumble sounding like the crashing of surf on a distant shore.

He pulled her onto his lap, one hand tracing circles on her back while the other slipped under her wool skirt to stroke her nylon-clad thigh. His fingers moved without shame, steadily upward under the cover of her skirt, and Julia's head fell back against the hard line of his shoulder as she arched in instinctive response.

Her hips strained to meet his touch, while the shifting of her body increased his own arousal until Marc thought he'd explode from the powerful force of his need. Small, soft whimpers of pleasure escaped her parted lips, the sound flaming his desire until he was seriously considering ways to take her right here, on the front seat of her compact car, in broad daylight, outside the bank.

It was that rather tawdry idea that jerked his mind back to reality and forced Marc to honestly consider his feelings for Julia. Could he actually still love her? Impossible. Marc Castellano did not carry a torch for any woman. No, the only reason he hadn't been able to erase her sultry image from his mind all these years was his oath to pay her back in kind. Nothing more . . .

But when he'd just about decided to take her to the nearest motel and satisfy this burning need, Julia's soft sob of surrender against his lips pulled an emotional cord far stronger than his animosity. Marc knew she was his for the taking. But he couldn't do it. Not like this.

He forced his hand to abandon its sweet quest and took a long breath, releasing it wearily. "Julia, I'm sorry . . . I really am."

Julia looked up at him, her eyes turning hard as reality flooded in to replace the soft glow of desire.

"Are you really? How thoughtful." Her tone was filled with self-loathing as she twisted her hands together in her lap. "Look, Marc, why don't you just make a decision about whether you want to give Apollo's account to my bank and leave me alone? Or are you getting some kind of kinky thrill watching me fall apart every time you come within ten feet of me?"

At her bitter tone, a muscle jumped in his dark cheek, but Marc managed to keep his composure. "Of course I'm not enjoying this. I realize that after what you did that summer, you might be expecting me to enjoy your pain, but it's never done anything but kill me to see you unhappy, Julia."

She stared at him, shaking her head in disbelief. "You're an amazing liar, Marc Castellano. Do you actually believe that? After what you did to me, I'm the one who should hate you."

"What I did to you? You mean making you a woman after you spent three weeks throwing your near-nude body in front of me every chance you got? You were begging me to make love to you, Julia, and I sure as hell don't remember you putting up much of a fight!"

She shrugged his hands from her shoulders. "I'm not talking about that," she retorted. "I'm talking about the way you conveniently disappeared, leaving me to face the inquisition. I told my parents that you loved me." Her gaze narrowed, her hazel eyes now blazing with fires of resentment. "But you proved differently, didn't you? I don't know why I should have been surprised, Marc. You showed about as much integrity as anyone would expect from a Castellano."

"I wish you hadn't said that, Julia." His voice was low, more dangerous than Julia had ever heard it.

Actually, watching the intense pain shadow his eyes, Julia also wished she'd refrained from that particular remark. She knew Marc had struck others for that indictment and realized it was taking a Herculean effort for him not to strike out at her, even if she was a woman. Pride kept her from admitting her regret as she met his eyes with a show of bravado, not realizing that her own anguish was evident in her eyes.

Marc broke the intense, stifling mood when his dark eyes cut down to his watch. "I have to go. I've got an appointment with the architects at four."

"That's fine with me."

"I'll pick you up at eight."

"But—" Her eyes flew to his face, surprised that he would still consider a social evening possible.

"We had a deal, Julia. And I don't welch, whatever you may think of the Castellanos."

Her hands were still twisted together in her lap and Marc sighed as he lifted them to his lips, unable to leave things like this. How could he be thinking about ruining her life when just damaging her afternoon made him feel as if he had a knife embedded between his ribs?

"I promise you, tonight there'll be no fighting. We'll pretend we're two strangers, going out on our first date. I don't know anything about you, except that I find you remarkable and breathtakingly beautiful. You don't know anything about me except that I'm devilishly obstinate and you've finally given in and granted me one date to prove how charming I can be. Then, Julia, we'll take it from there."

She shook her head with a sigh. "We can't go back, Marc. You can't go home again, didn't you ever read that?"

Damn. Why couldn't he maintain his resolve? Why couldn't the anger that had simmered within him all these years stay alive when he was with her?

"I don't want to go back, Julia, there's nothing for us there. I want to go forward. Let me at least give it a try."

As he drew her into the circle of his arms, caressing and soothing her with his gentle touch, Julia felt a strange lethargy creeping into her limbs. She rested her head against his shoulder, inhaling the scent of his woodsy after-shave. At this moment there was no more fight left in her and for the time being she decided not to dwell on might-have-beens. There was a significant little silence as she formulated her answer.

"All right, Marc . . . But make it eight-thirty, will you?

I always like to primp a little longer for a first date." She lifted her head to give him a wobbly, crooked smile.

"You never look anything but beautiful, Julia. But eight-thirty it is. And thank you."

He dropped a light kiss to her forehead. Another quick kiss to the tip of her nose, then her cheeks, had her quivering. The soft feathering along her lips was only an enticement, but Marc released her and left the car before she could open her eyes.

"Have a good afternoon," he said huskily, his shared smile indicating he knew very well how frustrated he'd left her body because his was suffering too.

"Thank you. Good luck with your architects."

Julia watched as he walked toward his own black Lotus, his long-legged movements possessing a predatory gracefulness. Then she lowered her forehead to the top rim of the steering wheel for a moment, to garner enough control of her wildly catapulting emotions to return to her office. She took several deep breaths, willing the rush of oxygen to her lungs to clear her head.

Eventually she regained her composure, repaired the ravages of the afternoon as best as she could, put on her glasses, and went back to work. As she walked across the asphalt parking lot, Julia failed to see Charles Stevenson leaving the window of his office, a blistering expression on his face.

Chapter Six

Julia found a message from George on her desk, asking her to drop by his office. By the time she reached the penthouse office of Silverado Fidelity Bank's president, she'd redonned her mask of a cool, competent banker.

"You wanted to see me?"

"I did," he replied with a welcoming smile. "Come, tell me how it went with Castellano. Did he succumb to your feminine charms and agree to move his money to our safekeeping?"

"You know I don't operate that way, George," she snapped, hating herself the moment the words had escaped.

He was only teasing, as he had so often before. Although Julia dressed for work in serious dark suits, mirror images of her male counterparts' attire, there was no concealing the soft, feminine curves of the woman's body under the banker's gray serge. The somber colors accentuated her porcelain complexion, giving her an air of fragility from time to time.

Appearances, however, could be deceiving, as many a man had discovered when he refused to take Julia Cassidy seriously. She could hold her own in any financial circle and was becoming well-known to the insiders on Wall Street.

"I'm sorry," George responded to her short tone with consummate grace, "I didn't mean to imply that your behavior was anything but professional."

"He still hasn't decided," Julia answered his question finally. "I don't know who our competition is, and that's got me working in the dark. If I only knew who else he'd talked to, I'd know which points to highlight. You and I know we can meet any offers other banks might make. I only hope I can convince Marc, uh, Mr. Castellano of that fact."

Julia cringed at her slip, but George seemed disinclined to pick up on it. "I'm sure you'll have no trouble. Oh, by the way, I've received the information on his source of revenue. The man is squeaky clean. He's built that business himself, relying on an incredible sense of intuition as to where the market is going to be a year from now. There's not a single sign of Castellano gambling money in Apollo Enterprises."

Julia picked up the thick, bound report, skimming through the pages. "I knew there wouldn't be," she answered softly.

"You sound as if you know him well."

Julia struggled to remember what she'd told George about her relationship with Marc, recalling that she'd mentioned their age differences as a barrier to anything but the most fleeting acquaintance.

"Not really," she lied unconvincingly. "But Marc Castellano isn't the only person in Reno who possesses intuition, George. I have a fair share myself."

He nodded. "Of course you do, Julia. A banker without those inborn instincts isn't going to succeed. Especially in today's marketplace."

She tapped her fingernail on the cover of the report.

"Those inborn instincts, George, are why I knew Marc Castellano was honest. I'll rely on those over country-club gossip any day." She grinned. "Especially when backed up by a twenty-page report."

She felt better now that they'd returned the conversation back to an area where she was in control. One of the reasons Julia enjoyed her work was the fact that she did have a knack for it. The Midas touch, some had dubbed her ability to know the market future so well. She was in control in this world of high finance.

The remainder of the afternoon flew by without a hitch, giving her a respite from the emotional buffeting she'd been experiencing. Even her computer, she noticed, behaved perfectly, its rebellious mood seeming to have been charmed by Marc's touch.

Who could blame it? she thought even as she shook her head with a wry regret. It was ridiculous, the way she was drawn to Marc Castellano. And yet, as ridiculous as it was, the idea didn't wipe the smile of anticipation from her lips as she tried to keep her mind on business rather than on the evening ahead.

"Would you care to know your problem?"

Julia looked up from a stack of ledgers, seeing Charles in the doorway. He was propped lazily against the door frame, his long legs clad in gray flannel slacks crossed at the ankles.

"I'll bite. What, exactly, is my problem?"

He entered her office with a loose-limbed stride, coming to sit on the corner of her desk, waving at the papers strewn over the lustrous patina of the wood.

"All this . . . You work too hard, darling."

Julia shook her head. A hairpin fell onto the sheet of paper and she picked it up, opening it with her front teeth before tucking the escaped tendril of hair back into the twist covering the nape of her neck.

"I'm an investment banker, Charles, attempting to operate in a time of constant flux. I need to be constantly studying the trends to find some pattern in this crazy financial world we've all been tossed into." She took off her glasses momentarily, folding the frames back and forth in an absent gesture as she looked up into his disapproving blue eyes. "What would you have me do? Tack the *Wall Street Journal*'s listing of stocks on a wall and throw darts?"

"That's not such a bad idea. Considering the law of averages, you'd probably do just fine. And have a lot more fun while you were at it."

"I have fun," Julia argued, shoving her glasses back onto her face. "I love my work, Charles. I find it exhilarating, fascinating, and totally fulfilling."

"Now you sound just like Dad," he muttered, sliding off the desk to pace the room.

His hands were curled into fists, thrust deeply into his front pockets. Julia was moderately surprised by the resentment brewing in his blue eyes as he turned toward her once more. But it did not amaze her as it might have last week. It was as if Marc's return to town had somehow tipped the world on its axis, causing everyone to act uncharacteristically.

George was walking about this place with the grinning, self-satisfied look of a cat that had just swallowed the canary, cage and all. Her behavior, of course, had been totally aberrant. And now Charles seemed to have come under a similar spell, discarding his usually unruffled temperament and showing a strain of disaffection toward his father and even herself. She put down her pen, replacing it with a cigarette. Charles immediately came to a halt beside her, bringing the flame of his gold lighter to the tip of the menthol cigarette.

"Christ, Julia, that's all I ever heard growing up. What

was good for this business. Banking isn't the end-all of this world. Hell, it isn't even fun."

"Perhaps that's why they call it work."

Charles expelled an exasperated sigh, throwing his body into a leather armchair. He slumped down, long legs stretched out in front of him, his gaze meeting hers across the top of her desk.

"Sometimes I think that Dad would be a lot happier if you were the only child in the Stevenson household instead of me. Just think how he could have spent your formative years playing bank with you . . .

"I can see it all now. Instead of that playhouse your parents built, you could have had a little bank building, with teller's cages, ledger sheets, safe-deposit boxes. I wonder if *Weekly Reader* put out a financial edition?"

"What did you want, Charles?" Julia's tone was brisk. She didn't know what in the world had Charles so peevish, but enough was enough.

"That's right." He expelled a huge, petulant sigh. "Back to work, right?"

"Right."

"All right. I came by to ask if you wanted to go out tonight."

"I can't," she replied instantly, returning her attention deliberately to the papers in front of her.

"I really need your help, Julia. I've gotten into a game at the Lodestone."

Julia mentally shook her head at the mention of the gambling casino known for its high-stakes poker games. When would Charles ever realize that he was a terrible cardplayer?

"You know I never gamble, Charles," she murmured, making a few notes in the margin of a file on offshore drilling interests.

"I just want you along to bring me luck," he pressed with a smile.

Julia laughed lightly. "How many times have you dragged me to one of those damnable card games and lost your shirt? You should realize by now that I'm not much of a talisman."

"Come on, Julia, be a sport," he urged, leaning forward in the chair.

"Charles, you know I don't like your gambling. But if you insist on going, perhaps you would have better luck without me. Maybe I'm a jinx." She smiled an encouraging smile, attempting to tease him into better temper.

"All right, darling," he agreed with an unattractive petulance, rising from the chair and walking to the doorway. "But if I lose my shirt, it's going to be all your fault."

It was impossible to feel sorry for Charles when he reverted to his childhood behavior of placing blame for all his misfortunes on someone else's shoulders.

"Just don't lose your pants," she called after him. "I'd hate to have to come bail you out of jail after you'd been picked up for indecent exposure."

Julia's hazel eyes followed him down the hallway for a moment, wishing she could call him back. She had the uneasy feeling she'd hurt his feelings, but how could she have done otherwise? Charles was an odd son for a banker. He was constantly seeking the quick score, the fast and easy money that would make up for all the losses. The problem was, of course, each time he needed a bigger win to cover the previous loss. The situation had begun to snowball, and she knew that George had finally refused to loan his son any more money to cover his gambling debts.

Julia hated to think what would become of Silverado Fidelity once Charles took over. If he ran this bank like he did his own personal finances . . . Well, she could only wish George Stevenson a long and prosperous life.

Marc paced the floor, his grip tight on the telephone receiver. A towel was tucked around his waist, and his jet hair gleamed with moisture from the shower.

"I agree, Brian. It looks damn suspicious."

"What time will you be arriving in Palo Alto, Marc? I'll meet the plane personally with all the data."

"Not until tomorrow morning, I'm afraid. I've got some loose ends to tie up here."

"Tomorrow morning!" Brian Huhn, Apollo Enterprises' research director, couldn't hide his disbelief. "Marc, do we have a bad connection? I thought I heard you say you wouldn't be back until tomorrow morning."

Marc stopped his marathon pacing in front of a triple-paned glass window, staring out at the lake, his attention momentarily diverted by a memory of Julia, frolicking in those crystal waters. God, she was lovely then. But now . . .

"Marc? Do I have your full attention?"

He shook his head to clear his thoughts. "Of course you've got it, Brian. And no, it's not a bad connection. I'll be back first thing in the morning, but that's as soon as I can make it. For the time being, you'll have to handle things on that end."

"Handle things? What the hell do you want me to do? Bob Manning in security sent some guys over to Murphy's house. He's disappeared, but there's plenty of evidence to indicate he's taken a bootleg copy of the EFT software with him, Marc."

Marc expelled a soft oath under his breath. This could be a major problem. Not just for Apollo Enterprises, but for every member bank tied into the network the new software program was designed to encode. He knew that

at this very moment he should be on a plane back to Palo
Alto. He'd built Apollo to world prominence by not
letting anything get in the way of his work, and he'd certainly never ignored an emergency for a woman, no matter how appealing she'd been.

Stupid, he told himself even as he was succumbing to
sensual memories of Julia, every minute counts. Marc
amazed himself, as well as Brian Huhn, with his ability to
shove that warning to the far reaches of his mind.

"You'd better call in the FBI, Brian," he stated. "And
have someone meet me at the executive terminal. I'll be
in at nine o'clock tomorrow morning."

His decision had the unmistakable ring of authority,
and although Marc knew his research director was dying
to argue his case for expediency one last time, Brian realized the futility of such an act. He agreed and hung up,
leaving Marc to wonder what the hell was happening to
his mind.

He was late. Julia had paced a marathon distance back
and forth across the lush ice-blue carpeting when the door-
bell finally rang. She forced herself to walk slowly and not
to run to answer it, as she so desperately wanted to.

"I'm sorry," he began as soon as she opened the door.
Marc's eyes widened as he stared at her, his rehearsed
apology forgotten.

Julia's warm hazel gaze was not idle as it moved over
him in turn. He looked so incredibly wonderful, the jet
of his hair repeated in the custom-tailored dinner jacket
and trousers. The pleated shirt was taut across his firmly
muscled chest, the black studs brightly polished.

Time was suspended. Words of contrition and absolu-
tion no longer held meaning. There was only this glorious, golden moment.

Marc's eyes gleamed with appreciation as they took a
leisurely tour, from the top of her flaming hair, across the

softened features of her face, down the slender column of her neck, to her bared, pearly-skinned shoulders. Julia's beaded gold dress was far removed from the image of a lady banker as one could ever hope to find. Strapless, it hugged her curves like a second skin. The long slit at the front of the floor-length skirt allowed movement, and also displayed a generous length of leg. The beam from her porch lamp was diffused as it hit the beads, the brilliant lights echoed in the golden strands lacing their way through her thick auburn hair. She'd piled it high atop her head, in a sophisticated style to match the dress, but already tendrils were escaping, curling down about her face, adding an endearing softness to her sleek image.

His gaze embodied the power of a physical caress, causing Julia to draw in a quick breath as it followed the slope of her breasts, his eyes narrowing, as if they were able to see through the beaded material. Desire heated his eyes as they moved over her curves, no less greedy than if the dress had been cast from molten gold and not merely metallic-toned beads.

Just when she thought she could no longer stand of her own accord, Marc was inside her living room, drawing her to him, burying his lips into her precariously restrained hair.

"I feel," he murmured, "as if I've just hit the jackpot."

He bent his head to taste Julia's lips with a leisurely restraint, as if he had all night to satisfy his thirst. Julia's mind was bombarded with sensual stimuli as her hands encircled his neck to play in the soft waves brushing the pristine white collar. His hair was like ebony silk, thick and luxurious to the touch.

His lips were firm, but caressingly tender at the same time, his broad white teeth nibbling at the full thrusting of her lower lip. His breath, as it wafted across her face, was a soft summer breeze, warm and sprigged with fresh mint. The scent of him, well-groomed and shaven, mingled with that tantalizing male essence she'd never been able to expunge from her memory.

It was as if Marc read her mind as he trailed his lips down her throat in nibbling little bites. "Lord, Julia, how I love that perfume on you. I can't think when I'm around you."

"Don't think," she gasped as his tongue flicked out to explore the hollowed shadow between her breasts. "Not now, Marc. Just hold me."

His palm pressed against the sensitive hollow of her lower back as his knee breeched the beaded material of her dress, sliding expertly into the long slit. Julia shifted against him, closing her eyes to the glorious communiqués his hard body was telegraphing to her with every sinuous thrust.

"Dinner." He groaned. "I've got dinner reservations and we're already late."

"I don't care," she whispered, her palms on either side of his face as she lifted his head to recapture his lips. "I'm not hungry, Marc."

Marc forced his shattered senses to remember the purpose to his plans this evening. "I am," he admitted. "And for a great deal more than dinner. But we have an agreement, Julia. And I intend to handle first things first." His hands released her to hang at his sides.

Marc's husky voice held a strange inflection and Julia tilted her head back, looking up into his dark, suddenly shuttered eyes. The smoldering desire was still apparent, but something else was slowly taking its place and she couldn't read the message.

"All right. I'd certainly hate to have you die of starvation before I can convince you to give me your account." Was that her voice? She'd never heard that weak tone in it before, certainly not when discussing business. She moved to her closet and pulled out the autumn ranch-mink coat, holding it out to him.

"Nice fur. A gift from Daddy?" Marc's voice was suddenly laced with scorn, and Julia lifted her chin defiantly.

"Of course not. I bought it myself with the commission I earned for bringing in Hudson Oil. It's not as impractical as it seems, Marc. You've obviously been away in sunny California for so long, you've forgotten how cold it gets up here."

"I haven't forgotten a thing about this place, Julia. Not how cold it gets . . . or how warm."

His pointed gaze took one last tour of her body, reminding her that she had always made it very warm and welcoming for him. Julia pulled the coat around her as if in self-defense.

Marc felt a sharp twinge of regret as her face grew very solemn and she withdrew behind the wall of animosity he'd initiated between them.

"Will we lose our reservations, do you think?" she asked, finally breaking the thick silence that had hovered over them in the cockpitlike interior of his car.

"No."

"You sound very sure of yourself, Marc. You've been away a long time. Perhaps you don't command as much respect as you once did." Julia slanted a tentative smile in his direction.

"This place I do," he muttered, his jaw tense, his gaze directed through the windshield.

He appeared disinterested in the conversation, and as the heavy silence settled down around them once more, Julia tried again. "Was it business that made you late this evening?"

"Yes." The single syllable was expelled through clenched teeth.

What in the world was the matter with the man? Just a

few minutes ago he'd held her in his arms, kissing her as if he'd never stop. Now it was as if she'd suddenly turned into Typhoid Mary.

"Marc? Are you angry at me?"

He shrugged. If there was one thing he wanted to forget, just for tonight, it was that Julia would be interested in discussing the theft of his EFT program. Right now he was far more interested in the sexy, seductive woman who dwelt within the cool, collected banker.

"No, Julia, I'm not angry. I've got a problem with Apollo, but I promise not to let it ruin our evening."

Her fingers stroked his thigh in a natural, caring gesture, and Marc had to grit his teeth, restraining his body's response.

"Is it something bad?"

He didn't want to talk about it. If they began discussing the program, they could conceivably waste precious hours discussing business. Christ, was there anything more boring than banking? But, on the other hand, was there any more desirable banker than Julia Cassidy?

His answer to Julia's inquiry, when it finally came, was short and uninformative. "I had a phone call shortly before leaving to pick you up. There's every reason to believe someone has stolen one of our more sensitive programs."

"Stolen? How could that be? Surely you have maximum security?"

"Of course we do. But there are other ways. Bribery, blackmail—you never know what will turn a normally honest individual into a traitor."

"You think someone in your organization is selling secrets?"

"It looks that way," he agreed grimly.

"We can do this some other time, Marc. Shouldn't you be getting right back to Palo Alto?"

Marc turned to her, his face sober for a moment as his gaze took in her sincerely concerned expression. Then he smiled, that heartbreakingly beautiful smile that had always possessed the ability to melt her bones.

"I've got something even more important to do tonight, Juliet. With you."

A blush warmed Julia's face at his suggestive words and she turned away to look out the window at the darkened landscape. He was driving toward the resort town of Stateline, on the southern shore of Lake Tahoe, and she suddenly realized where he planned to take her. She wasn't wrong. He pulled the low-slung car up in front of the private casino.

"Now I know why you weren't worried about losing your dinner reservations," she remarked. The casino was owned and operated by the Castellanos. Fat chance they'd give away a table belonging to one of their own.

Marc's black eyes were watchful as they held her gaze. "We can go somewhere else," he suggested, an obvious question in his voice.

Julia shook her head, rejecting his proposal. If this would finally prove to Marc that she was not the snob he thought she was, she would cheerfully eat dinner here every night for the rest of her life.

"We made a deal, Marc. I agreed to go anywhere you chose," she replied calmly.

Suddenly, this entire scheme seemed idiotic and Marc wished he could turn the damn car around and head back to Reno. "I know you did, but—"

She patted his cheek, smiling at him across the intimate interior of the Lotus. "But nothing. Now, if you don't mind, Mr. Castellano, I'm suddenly starving."

Once inside, Julia's hazel eyes swept through the private casino, awed by the dissimilarity between this ambience of subdued wealth and the glittery gambling dens of Reno she'd visited with Charles.

The hand-cut prisms of several crystal chandeliers sparkled in the high ceiling, so dissimilar to the flashing neon so usually associated with gambling. The walls were painted a rich jeweled ruby, the gloss so high that Julia had to run her fingers across the surface to realize they weren't covered in leather. The marble-patterned carpeting continued the elegance of the marble foyer, but effectively muffled the sounds in the room.

There was no grinding clatter of slot machines; this crowd was not into low-stakes gambling by any means. Where in the public casinos one could find an eclectic mix of customers, dressed in everything from faded jeans to designer original evening gowns, all pressed together around the rectangular craps table in total equality, here democracy had been abandoned for an atmosphere of elegant chic. The patrons at the gambling tables were expensively dressed, and the croupiers' custom-tailored tuxedos were every bit as elegant as those worn by their clients.

There were no exuberant exclamations as fortunes were won, nor mournful cries and expletives as others were lost; instead, there was only the steady hum of sub-dued voices.

While Julia's family could be considered wealthy on anyone's balance sheet, she knew they were a long, long way from assets held by the Castellanos' clientele. As her gaze moved over the quietly intent gamblers, she recognized several faces from all walks of life. Politicians, captains of industry, media stars—all were represented.

"The rich are different," she murmured. She allowed Marc to take the mink, giving it up to the attendant.

"Of course," he answered on cue, sotto voce, "they have more money."

Marc's hand rested lightly on her back as they followed the maître d' into a large, domed dining room already filled with patrons. Their table was across the vast room and heads swiveled, observing their entrance.

Once seated, with the wine ordered, Marc asked the question Julia had been expecting, his dark gaze intent as he studied her face. "Would you prefer a private room?"

Julia made him wait for his answer as she slowly unfolded the damask linen napkin and placed it on her lap. Lifting a crystal goblet to her lips, she drank the ice water slowly in an attempt to cool her rising temper. He could be so damn transparent. And irritating. And, she realized, choosing not to lash out at him, vulnerable. Why couldn't he see that it didn't matter? The differences in their families had never mattered, from the first moment she'd seen him.

"Not at all," she replied at length. "In fact, I see a table vacant in the middle of the room. I'm sure if you ask, the maître d' will move us. Then everyone will see that Julia Cassidy is dining with the notorious Marc Castellano. Would that make you feel any better?"

He fiddled with his silverware, which was sterling, she noted irrelevantly. The silence eddied around them as he rubbed at a nonexistent spot on his salad fork.

Damn. What was it about her that had him constantly behaving like an insecure adolescent? In the real world, the world of Apollo Enterprises, the name "Marc Castellano" meant something. It stood for strength, power, and success. But in the sensuous realm in which he moved with Julia Cassidy, it seemed he was constantly acting like an absolute idiot.

"I guess I laid it on a bit heavily, didn't I?"

"With a trowel," Julia agreed dryly.

"Would you believe that I'm sorry . . . and that I'm willing to leave, right now?"

She reached out, covering his hand with hers. "You're the man who's starving, remember? Let's just order and enjoy the evening."

Marc's eyes were still wary as he studied her, but he only nodded in agreement and opened the tasseled menu.

The dinner was delicious, as Julia had expected in such an establishment, and the wine was an excellent vintage. They were savoring their coffee, which she noted with some amusement was Marc's blend, when Joe Castellano strode up to their table. A hard, compact man in his late sixties, he was shorter than Marc by a great deal, more typical of Sicilian men, but he possessed the same midnight-black hair, which in his case was streaked with silver. His eyes were hard, resembling stones, as they flicked over Julia, failing to exhibit the human tenderness so often visible in Marc's gaze.

"Marco," he greeted his nephew warmly, "it's good to have you home again." Joe's voice was harsh and scratchy, but anyone could tell there was honest affection in the greeting.

A lifelong bachelor, he'd done his best to take over Marc's upbringing after Sam and Angie's car had skidded on the icy highway and careened off the cliff at the exact spot that was now a spectacular viewpoint overlooking the lake.

He'd entrusted Marc's religious and secular education to the nuns, but it was here, at the Castellano family casino during summer vacations, that Marc learned about life. When he was eight, Marc discovered he had an affinity for poker. By the summer he was twelve, he was consistently beating his uncle and the casino's best dealers in private games held in the back room. At fourteen, he'd mastered blackjack, his eidetic memory and mathematical flair enabling him to easily count cards. At sixteen, a friendly chorus girl introduced him to sex, and for the remainder of that summer Marc's interests had turned from numbers to more pleasurable pursuits.

"I'm glad to be back, Uncle Joe," Marc answered. "I like the Silicon Valley well enough, but I've felt like an ex-patriot all these years. It's hard to get the beauty of this country out of your system."

"Don't I know," the older man agreed in a fervent voice. "It was a crime you left in the first place."

With that, he turned in Julia's direction, his gaze as dark as the freshly brewed beverage she was sipping. But his eyes held all the warmth of iced coffee and she slowly lowered the cup to the gold-rimmed saucer.

Marc broke the charged silence. "Julia Cassidy, this is my uncle, Joseph Castellano. Uncle Joe, Julia."

"I'm pleased to meet you," she said, extending her hand.

Joseph Castellano could not refuse to shake her hand, but he did allow a pause before doing so that extended a heartbeat longer than good manners dictated.

"It's always a pleasure to meet one of Marco's friends," he stated, insincerity obvious in his tone.

Julia stared as he turned and walked away, his broad back as stiff as steel.

Marc took her hand in his, lacing their fingers together. "Dance with me."

Julia's attention was still directed to the man across the room, but at the warmth in Marc's tone, she rose slowly from the table and they moved onto the nearly deserted dance floor.

He pulled her into his arms, his hand resting lightly on her bare skin as they moved idly to the music of a jazz quartet.

"I'm sorry about that. He promised he'd try." Marc's tone held a note of contrition.

"He's not exactly Mr. Personality, is he?" She turned her head to see Joe Castellano speaking with enthusiasm to a couple at another table. His smiling face was a distinct contrast to the stern mask she'd been offered.

Marc's fingers slid into the low-cut back of her dress, lightly massaging the delicate bones at the base of her spine. One knee slid into the deep slit, nudging against her thigh with an erotic message. His firm lips were arousingly close to her ear, his breath a warm caress on her skin as he sought to explain his uncle's behavior.

"He's got to learn that I want you and I don't care how he feels about it. Don't worry, he'll come around." Marc smiled down at her, his eyes clouding as they focused on her lips—full pink lips that parted on a gasp as he brought her more intimately into the embrace.

Her eyes were open invitations, which Marc readily accepted, lowering his dark head so his lips could meet hers. His tongue slid silkily into the velvet interior, brushing tantalizingly along the sensitive roof of her mouth, causing lightning to flash behind her closed lids.

They were touching, from the cling of their lips, to their thighs, their bodies fitting together in superb unity. Just when it seemed they'd go up in flames from spontaneous combustion, Marc returned to sanity, breaking the kiss to rest his chin on the top of her head.

"Another minute of that, and Uncle Joe would have had himself an X-rated floor show." His voice was ragged, laced with a mingling of desire and self-directed amusement. "As much as I hate to give up any opportunity to hold you in my arms, I only have a limited amount of self-restraint, and we've just about burned through it, Juliet. . . . Want to have a go at the tables?"

"I don't gamble," Julia answered automatically, her mind returning to his statement before he kissed her. "What do you mean, your uncle doesn't approve?"

"It doesn't matter," he insisted, his hand resting higher on her back now as they left the dance floor. "Neither one of us is a kid any longer, Julia. We don't need our families' permission to love each other."

Love? The word reverberated through her brain, ricocheting until Julia felt the entire room must have heard it. Her legs were lead as she stared up at him, wary eyes searching for the truth.

It was as if the years had fallen away when Julia and Marc's gaze met and held. The crystal teardrops from the chandelier overhead caught the shimmering rays of incandescent lights, splitting them into rainbows that reflected in their startled gazes.

Marc was as surprised to have uttered that statement as Julia had been to hear it, and for a moment neither moved, unable to break the silken net that had settled over them.

Chapter Seven

❧

Finally, with a jolt, Marc dragged his dark eyes from Julia's startled gaze and turned away, heading toward the felt-topped gambling tables.

Julia followed him blindly, her mind still on his words. She hadn't been surprised at her father's anger when he had discovered her relationship with Marc Castellano, but it had never entered her mind that his family might have any objections to her. She'd been too young for him, perhaps. But that certainly didn't explain the animosity etched into Joe Castellano's stony face this evening.

As for love—had he meant it? But even if he did, the word obviously held a far different meaning for Marc than it did for her.

"Here. Hold out your hands."

Julia was shaken from her troubled thoughts when Marc dropped a pile of colored chips into her hands.

"I told you I don't gamble," she objected.

"Everyone gambles," he replied easily, leading her to one of the tables. "Life is a gamble, Julia."

"Not mine," she insisted.

Marc stopped for a moment, staring down at her, his

expression inscrutable. "Then perhaps it's time you began," he suggested softly.

She recognized his tone of voice, which reminded her of her agreement to spend the evening any way he wished. She shrugged. "All right. But I'm warning you, Marc, I'll probably end up losing every one of these stupid chips."

"Have a little faith in Lady Luck, Julia. We'll begin with roulette," he decided, leading her toward the spinning wheel. "Even a mental midget can learn that right off."

Julia stopped dead in her tracks, tilting her chin upward as she met his teasing gaze dead on. "I am definitely not a mental midget, Marc Castellano. I may not be into high-tech electronics, creating all sorts of Frankensteinian monsters, but I do have a damn good head on my shoulders."

"Mmm. And such delicious shoulders they are, sweetheart," he murmured, bending to brush his lips over her smooth skin.

"Marc, we were discussing my intelligence. Not my body."

"I know. It's just that if you want to keep a man's mind on your brain, Julia, you should never pour yourself into a dress that calls out to his more primitive instincts." His lips blazed a trail from her shoulders down her bare back and up again, nibbling at her neck.

Julia twisted out of his light embrace, damning the trembling of her awakened body. "Would you remember we're in a public place?"

"This was a dumb idea," he muttered, heaving a frustrated sigh. "I should have forgone the test and just served you an intimate little dinner at my place. Then I could kiss your slender neck, these pearly shoulders, this graceful back, and all those other, even more delectable portions of your lovely body." His fingers lightly brushed the trail he had in mind, and Marc realized he was dabbling in masochism.

A low, controlled voice shattered the romantic moment, and Julia started, her eyes wide as she looked with despair at the long green felt. She belatedly realized that the tuxedoed man at the wheel had been speaking to her.

"Marc?"

"Choose a number, sweetheart," he suggested, his firm lips curved in an encouraging grin, his head tilting in the direction of the table.

"I don't know . . ." Julia vacillated, the decision seeming unreasonably important, considering the fact that the chips didn't even seem like real money. Her eyes swept across the numbers, her bottom lip caught unconsciously between her teeth.

There was a murmur of impatience from the other players, but the man waited, unwilling to rush any guest of Marc Castellano.

"Pick a color, then, Julia," Marc suggested. "That way there are only two choices."

That was easier. There was only one possible choice. Black, the color of Marc's lustrous hair and his wonderful eyes. She placed a single chip on the expanse of green, ignoring his deep chuckle.

"A reckless woman," he teased her. "Your daring overwhelms me, sweetheart. At this rate it'll take you all night to lose those chips."

Marc's eyes were spiked with humor as he observed Julia's tense stance, her taut body directed in a line toward the finally spinning roulette wheel.

"Hush," she scolded him, not taking her eyes off the bouncing ball. "You're interfering with my concentration."

He put his arms about her waist and drew her against him in a friendly, undemanding manner.

"I won!" Julia clapped her hands with childish glee as the ball settled with a rattle into the slot occupied by the black number eleven. It didn't matter to her in the least that the other patrons were looking at her with amusement. The reward came when the banker returned her chip, as well as another matching one.

"I'm going to do it again," she decided, placing another chip on black.

"Why don't you put two down?" Marc suggested.

"Because I don't want to lose."

"But you won't really be losing. You'll be betting one of your own and the one you just won, honey," he coaxed her.

The banker waited, his face a study in uninvolvement as they held up the play once again.

"Please, Marc, you'll make me nervous," she stated firmly, nodding to the man that she was ready.

When the ball once again dropped into a black slot, this time number thirty-five, Julia was ecstatic, and ready to spread her wings a bit more. Marc bit back the laugh as she placed two chips on black.

Three hours later, becoming more intrepid, she'd moved onto numbers, winning consistently. It didn't take long before she had grown absolutely lionhearted, escalating her odds as she played emotional hunches every time. Marc's age. The date she met him. The date he returned into her life. His birthday. Any numbers she could switch around to remotely relate to him. She won each time, the pile of chips growing higher and higher.

"Want to cash them in and go home?" Marc murmured into her ear as she grinned saucily at the banker and pushed a pile of chips onto six—the first digit in the Lotus' license plate.

"But, Marc, I'm getting so lucky," she said, leaning over the table to watch the ball as it spun in the polished wheel.

"I know. But I was hoping for a little luck myself tonight."

His deep voice held an unmistakable invitation and Julia glanced over her shoulder, her face flushed with excitement. Her exuberant features softened slightly as their gaze held and she lifted her hand to his cheek.

"You're right," she agreed softly. "It's late. And we both have a long day tomorrow."

"Today," he corrected, casting yet another glance at his watch.

"Today? Have I been playing that long?"

"You have. For someone who never gambles, darling, you caught on very well."

"We'll go now," she stated, turning around in time to watch the ball settle into the groove numbered with a six.

She waited in the foyer as Marc cashed in her chips. "What in the world is this?" Julia stared at the stack of bills he placed in her hand.

"Your winnings, sweetheart."

"My winnings? How much is here?"

"Oh, somewhere in the neighborhood of twenty thousand dollars," he replied blithely, settling her coat over her shoulders and opening the door.

It had been warm in the casino and the blast of icy autumn air struck her face. Still, it was not as shocking as all this money.

"Twenty thousand dollars?" she squeaked.

"In the neighborhood. It's a bit more than that, actually."

"That's some neighborhood, Marc." She shoved the bills toward him. "I can't take this."

"Of course you can. You won it, honey. And don't

worry, with that crowd, twenty thousand certainly isn't going to break Uncle Joe."

"But it's too much," she protested, relieved when the attendant brought the Lotus and she could sink into the leather bucket seat.

"Enjoy it. Do something crazy," Marc suggested, shifting the car into gear.

"I did something crazy already. That's my problem," she complained. "How in the world did I win so much money?"

"It's not hard to do when you're betting with hundred-dollar chips," Marc stated calmly, pulling out of the parking lot and heading the sports car toward the California side of the lake.

"Marc Castellano! You were letting me bet with hundred-dollar chips?"

When he looked at her, his puzzlement was etched into his moonlit features. "Sure. What did you think they were?"

"I don't know. I suppose a dollar. At the most five."

The laugh exploded from within, deep and heartfelt. "In that place? You're a gem, Julia Cassidy. You've got all the attributes of a very desirable woman while managing to maintain a naïveté that's so fresh you're like a breath of spring."

There had been times that summer when Marc had seemed far more worldly than she. Back then, Julia had attributed it to age, but now she realized there was still that difference between them. They were opposites attracting with a force so strong as to prove the law of physics once and for all.

"You don't have to laugh at me," she snapped.

"I'm not laughing at you," he said, suddenly serious. "I was just trying to tell you that I've never met anyone like you. Believe me, I've tried. But it was an impossible quest."

His hand covered hers, his long fingers squeezing hers slightly. "Please keep the money. It's only a way to keep score. You could have just as easily lost it all."

She gasped, suddenly realizing the truth of his words. Reno was known as "the biggest little city in the world." And while all too often looked down upon as nothing but an imitation of Las Vegas, the town possessed many of the same qualities of its famous neighbor to the south. The casinos offered everything from nickel slot machines to the high-stakes games offered in the private clubs. The glitter lit the night sky; the air was static with expectation, desperation, and tragedy.

Gambling seemed to strip people of their veneer, she'd noticed long ago, choosing not to succumb to the temptations. Rich or poor, the chances were all the same when they stood up to gaming tables, people could come away with all the chips or just as easily lose them.

Julia had never wanted to take such risk—in the casinos or in her life. Before tonight, she'd only gambled once, that summer with Marc. And like so many other expectant visitors to Reno, she'd lost everything.

"I'll make you a deal," she said.

Marc turned toward her, arching his dark brow inquisitively.

"If we're going to have any kind of relationship, it has to be on an equal basis. You staked me, Marc, so I insist you take half the winnings." Her tone was firm.

"Fair enough."

Julia's hazel eyes narrowed. "You make me a little nervous when you're so agreeable. What's the catch?"

He patted her knee. "No catch, sweetheart. Haven't you figured out that I'm basically a very agreeable guy?"

Julia crossed her arms over her chest. "Humph.

You're also an expert at overstatement, Marc Castellano. I've yet to see one sign of your complaisance. And I still can't believe you're not putting up a fight about taking the money."

Marc shook his head. "You'll get no argument from me." Then he laughed. "Besides, you can't control how I spend it. My share is going for extravagant gifts for a sexy lady banker."

Julia shook her head in amused frustration, turning her gaze out the window, watching the towering pines flash by. When they passed the sign welcoming them to California, she knew without a doubt where Marc was taking her. To their place. That summer they'd spread a blanket over fallen pine needles, finding stolen bliss in each other's arms. But it was far too cold for such activities now. Julia wondered if he'd ever built on the property.

Her question was answered as he pulled the car up in front of a two-story mountain chalet, nestled in a grove of pine trees. The house was far from the main road, effectively secluded in the forest.

"Everything's changed," she whispered, looking around at the house, trees that she knew to be taller, and the lake beyond, which was deep and black in the darkness.

Marc reached out, taking her chin in his fingers as he gently turned her head toward him. "No, Juliet," he said on a husky timbre, "nothing's changed. And I'm going to prove that to you now."

Marc was out of the car, and opening Julia's door before she could think of a single argument. The cold wind promised the advent of winter and Julia drew her coat tighter. Since Marc's land was far away from the activity spawned by the gambling on the Nevada side of the lake, it was possible to believe they were the only two people in the world.

That's what she'd felt all those years ago: that this was a secret, magical place, removed from the cares of everyday life. The sun had always shone a little brighter out here, the water gleamed a deeper sapphire, and the stars glistened like loose-cut diamonds. She glanced upward at the brilliance of the night sky.

"I told you it hasn't changed," he murmured, his arm around her shoulder as she looked up at the pinpoints of light.

"But we have, Marc."

"No!" His exclamation was harsh. "I refuse to believe that." His arm tightened, impelling her against him for a silent, desperate moment. Then he squared his shoulders and managed an encouraging smile. "Come in and look around. I think you'll recognize the place."

Recognize the place? How in the world could she do that? Fifteen years ago the space occupied by Marc's house had been nothing but a stand of ponderosa pine. Julia watched as he pushed a button on the door. She could hear the mechanical noises of a lock being unbolted; then, as if by magic, the heavy door swung inward. Before she could question that strange occurrence, a whirring of gears had Julia spinning in the direction of an oddly familiar voice.

"Good evening, Mr. Castellano. Good evening, Ms. Cassidy," the low tones offered politely.

"Marc?" Julia's eyes widened as she searched for the source.

"Don't worry. It's just SAM."

"SAM?"

"Sight Activated Memory," he explained calmly. "Come on in, honey, and I'll introduce you."

Marc laced his fingers through Julia's, leading her

down a few steps into an alcove off the living room. There, resting on a broad pine table, was a computer not much larger than the small desktop units used at the bank. The difference, however, was the single camera lens that was observing them with unblinking attention.

"SAM's programmed to open the door. . . . There's a camera outside," Marc answered her astonished look.

Julia had the uneasy feeling Marc was pulling her leg. "Did you bring me all the way out here just to play a practical joke on me, Marc? This is impossible." She looked up at him. "Isn't it?"

"It's not a practical joke. Nor is it a trick. And believe me, Julia, SAM is *not* why I brought you here tonight."

Caught up in the problem of SAM, Julia missed Marc's seductive invitation. He was beginning to wish he'd given SAM the night off as she continued to stare at the computer.

"But how in the world can he tell one person from another? Or a person from a raccoon, for that matter?"

Marc placed his finger over her lips, grinning as he turned her toward the living room. "Shh, don't insult his intelligence or you might not be allowed in next time."

"But Marc," Julia argued, taking a seat on the first piece of furniture she came to, "you can't expect me to believe something that's straight out of Disneyland."

She glanced around, taking in the room. It seemed oddly familiar, but for the moment she wasn't interested in his house, which had obviously been custom-designed.

"Tell me the truth," Julia insisted. "You've got someone stashed away, watching a hidden monitor and speaking through a microphone."

Marc's lips quirked with ill-concealed amusement. "Nope. Would you care for a drink? Brandy, perhaps?"

"That would be nice," she agreed absently, her brow furrowed. "If he *is* real, how did he know my name?"

Marc's back was to her as he poured the dark-amber liquor into the crystal balloon glasses.

"Easy. I showed him some old pictures of you. I'll admit I had some reprogramming to do after your secretary introduced you as *Ms.* Cassidy. I had him trained to call you Julia."

Julia turned to stare back at the now-silent computer, shaking her head in a bemused fashion. Marc always had possessed an eccentric sense of humor. This simply had to be a joke.

"I still don't believe it," she declared.

Marc crossed the room in long strides, a glass in each hand. "What don't you believe? The fact that SAM exists, or that I've taught him manners?"

"I've never heard of any computer like that." She took the glass he offered, holding it between her palms as her gaze remained directed on SAM. *My God, he's even got me thinking of it by that stupid name.* She knew it was a joke and waited impatiently for the punch line.

"That's because he's not marketable yet," Marc explained. "He's a test model, and although I'm moderately pleased with SAM's intelligence, he's got a long way to go before he can begin earning his keep."

He settled down on the sofa, stretching one arm along the top as he turned toward her. "Now, let's forget about SAM and talk about us," he suggested, his finger brushing along her shoulder.

Julia turned back in the direction of the computer, missing Marc's muffled sigh of frustration. "Can he really see?"

"Some things," Marc answered with a patient resignation he didn't feel.

"If it's really not a trick, then tell me how you do it," she instructed firmly, doubt still lacing her voice.

"All right. SAM's electronic eye breaks an image into squares and assigns a number to each, depending on the intensity of its light reflection. He then compares the numbers with others in his memory, to determine whether what he's viewing is, let's say, a car or a person."

"But he knew our names."

"Do you realize that I'm beginning to feel like the guy who brought his best girl home and discovered she was falling in love with his roommate?"

Julia ran her finger around the top of the glass, looking thoughtfully into the depths. Swirling it, she absently watched the amber waves rock against the crystal sides.

"I'm sorry, Marc. I always knew you were intelligent, but I have to admit, I'd never suspected anything like this. Tell me how he knew my name."

"SAM is a new prototype of a parallel computer that can absorb enough simultaneous sensory stimulations to recognize a face. He's very accurate, and I believe future generations will have the capacity to make decisions or draw their own inferences on who's facing the machine. At this point, he only knows to open the door for you or me. For everyone else, it remains locked."

"I'm truly impressed, Marc." She issued the understatement softly.

"Don't be until you see this, honey."

Marc grinned, taking her hand as he led her back to the alcove where SAM seemed to be waiting, his single camera eye gazing at them solemnly.

Don't be fanciful, Julia scolded herself. He's not some humanoid. He's not even cute.

"Why doesn't he look like a robot? I certainly don't want to hurt your feelings, Marc, but SAM isn't very cute."

"You mean like R2D2?

"Yes. This looks like any normal computer. Except for his eye, of course . . . or his lens . . . or whatever you call it."

Marc laughed with pleasure, bending down to brush a light kiss on the tip of her nose. Julia held her breath, waiting for the feathery caress to continue downward to her lips, but Marc broke it off. She was beginning to realize she was in the company of a man of uncommon brilliance, yet at this moment, his expression was that of a young boy showing off his latest collection of *Star Wars* gadgetry.

"The people who will eventually be purchasing SAM aren't interested in *cute*, honey. They're interested in results."

A smile tugged at the corners of her mouth. "Oh, I see. You're always the pragmatic scientist, huh?"

"Right."

Her grin broke loose, echoed by the teasing glint in the golden flecks of her hazel eyes. "Then, why did you bother to name him? Or call *it* a *him*? You've got a lot of nerve, Marc Castellano, teasing me about *my* paranoia concerning *my* computer. The only names I've ever given him are Anglo-Saxon ones, when he hides my files like he did this morning."

Marc smiled back somewhat sheepishly. "Caught me. I'll admit to anthropomorphizing from time to time. Computer research gets a little lonely, sweetheart. It's nice to have some company in the lab."

"I'm surprised that you didn't name it Samantha," she teased.

"If I'd been into female names," Marc countered, his eyes bright with insinuation, "I'd have named it Julia. But we've already determined that you're an original." Marc turned back to the computer, missing the soft, pleased flush his words had encouraged. "Now, please stop arguing and watch."

He covered SAM's camera eye with a black cloth. "Stand in front of him."

Julia followed Marc's instructions, feeling distinctly uneasy as she waited for whatever would happen next.

"Hello, Ms. Cassidy," the deep voice repeated in a voice that sounded amazingly like Marc's, but more mechanical. "Welcome home."

Her hazel eyes widened as they flew from the black-covered lens to Marc's face. "How in the world—?"

"Your perfume," he enlightened her, as if the capability of a computer to recognize Shalimar was not at all unusual.

"You're not telling me this thing has a bionic nose?"

"Of sorts."

There was a hint of apology in Marc's tone at SAM's limitations as he continued to explain. "Right now he only begins to approach the capabilities of a human nose, which possesses millions of smell-receptor cells. SAM only has a few thousand individual odor receptors connected to one microchip. Each individual scent produces the same electrical voltage response each time. Shalimar, I have to admit, was a toughie. It has sandalwood, spice, and flowers in an amber base. It took a long time to isolate all the scents."

"You did that?" Julia inquired, her voice soft. "Why?"

Marc had asked himself that same nagging question over the years as he'd struggled with the problem. He knew the concept possessed great marketability. The perfected device, while admittedly not needing the ability to detect the scent of various perfumes, could determine the alcoholic content of a drunk driver, uncover the presence of explosives in an aircraft, or monitor pollution. That was his intent. Yet, he'd labored over that silly formula, experiencing a surge of exhilaration when SAM had ultimately responded to the enticing Oriental scent.

"I don't know," he admitted, looking a bit self-conscious. "All I do know is that it's taken the past five years to program SAM for scents. And you never left my mind during that time, Julia. Nor the ten years before that."

"Oh, Marc." Julia's eyes glazed with a sudden hint of tears as she looked up into his face. She loved him. She'd always loved him. To know that he'd been thinking of her during the years of separation was an incredible revelation. Marc had been right. Nothing had changed. This wooded hideaway still held the magic to banish the outside world and let love bloom freely.

"God, how I want to make love to you, Juliet," he whispered, his eyes locked to her misty hazel ones.

"Funny you should mention that, Marc." Julia's voice was tinged with a slight breathlessness. "Because that's precisely what I want, too."

Marc exhaled a sigh of aching pleasure as he drew Julia to him, his hands deftly dispensing with the pins that held her hair in precarious order. His hurried gestures allowed the thick auburn waves to tumble down, drifting over her shoulders in a soft, fiery cloud.

"I've always loved your hair down," he murmured, bending his head to press his lips against her perfumed tresses.

God, there wasn't an inch on her body that didn't exude her gloriously tenacious scent. It was a wonder poor SAM hadn't shorted out with the exquisitely voluptuous perfume. Marc knew he was close to exploding himself.

"It's too uncontrollable," she answered, her voice faltering as his warm breath stirred the loose strands framing her temple. "I swear the stuff has a mind of its own."

"Not unlike the lovely lady it adorns, sweetheart." Marc's hands slipped under the open mink coat, sliding around to her back as he pressed her firmly into his aroused strength. His lips covered hers in a gentle promise and Julia held on to his shoulders to steady herself.

"Marc, not here, please," she objected softly, twisting her head slightly to escape his lips.

Marc's mouth went dry and there was a husky catch to his deep voice. "Why not, Julia? This is our place. I built it for us. No other woman has ever been here."

Julia didn't have time to fully acknowledge that amazing thought as Marc's hands and lips and body all urged her to abandon her protest.

"Not this house," she gasped as his tongue eased along the shell-like convolutions of her ears, "it's this room. I can't with . . . with *him* watching us."

Marc's laugh of relief was full-bodied. "Now you're the one with the anthropomorphizing problem. Besides, SAM's eye is already covered. But I've got a more comfortable spot in mind, anyway."

He scooped her up into his arms as if she were nothing but a soft pile of feathers, and carried her up the spiral stairway to his bedroom.

Chapter Eight

❧

Marc lowered Julia almost reverently to the bed, his lips clinging to hers with uncommon hunger. The mattress sank under his weight as he sat down and slipped the mink coat from her shoulders. Her wide-eyed beauty stirred ancient fires in his loins and he fought for control, fighting down the urge to take her in one blinding surge of passion. He'd waited fifteen years for this night and he wanted it to be perfect in every way.

"I've never forgotten anything about you, Julia. I've spent years remembering you just this way." His hands trembled ever so slightly as he lifted a strand of her hair, trailing it along the line of her collarbone with a slow, sensuous touch. "I've never forgotten how your hair reminds me of flames. It's a wonder it doesn't burn your skin.

"I've imagined your eyes, soft as the mist over the lake in the morning, except when you want me. Then they flare with golden sparks that warm me to the core." His lips brushed her sensitive eyelids.

Julia shivered slightly at the erotic caress, her submission causing Marc to feel both wildly victorious and infinitely tender at the same time.

"I've gone crazy remembering your lips, Juliet. Sweet as vintage wine, and every bit as intoxicating."

Julia felt the shudder course through Marc's taut body as his mouth lightly covered hers, and she realized he was utilizing every bit of his self-restraint. His eyes were dark pools of hunger when he finally dragged his mouth away.

"Shall I go on?"

"Please do," she encouraged with a suddenly shy smile, grateful for the way he was bridging the chasm of intervening years, banishing their separation with his low, seductive tones. She was bathed in a golden warmth as she lay still under his gaze.

Marc's deep voice was ragged with desire as he moved to obey her softly issued request. He swallowed a moan of impatience, forcing himself to go slowly.

"Your skin . . . God, you have no idea how many times I've awakened at night, desperate for the feel of this satiny skin next to mine."

His devastating fingers trailed across her shoulders, and his palms brushed the upswell of her breasts. They were smooth now, Julia noticed through the sensual mist surrounding them. When Marc was younger, those same palms had had calluses from the hard work he'd done for his uncle.

Despite the difference in texture, however, their ability to drive her wild prevailed. She threw back her head and closed her eyes, concentrating on every blazing sensation imparted by the increasing intimacy of his touch.

The zipper at the back of her dress was no challenge. Julia kept her eyes closed, tawny lashes resting on her flushed cheeks as she felt him slide the heavy beaded gold dress down her body. Her strapless bra, slip, and panty hose followed in short order.

"Julia, look at me," Marc instructed in a hoarse voice.

Unable to deny him anything, she fluttered her hazel eyes open, and was stunned by the raw hunger on his face.

"I want to make it good for you, Julia. Better than it's ever been."

No, he amended as his pulse pounded in his veins, he wanted more than that. He wanted to love her. Lord, how he wanted that! But as he gazed down at her glistening, fragrant flesh, he felt like a pagan conqueror, intent on claiming foreign territory.

He wanted to expunge for all time any memory she may hold of any other man. He wanted to scorch away the lingering touches left by any male hands, the taste of any male lips. He wanted to claim Julia as his own so that if another man dared to touch her, she would feel his own touch instead. If any lips ever attempted to drink from hers, the taste of Marc Castellano would come between them. And if she ever dared to make love with any other man, she'd find her bed already claimed by his presence.

His hands were doing wickedly wonderful things to her body, causing Julia to shiver with delight. Her own hands moved between them, her fingers fumbling with the black studs on his shirt.

"Don't worry about that, Marc," she replied on a desperate thread of sound. "Just worry about how to get you out of these damn clothes."

His deep chuckle rumbled from his chest as he stood up, pulling off the black bow tie and flinging it carelessly onto a chair.

"Watch carefully, woman, while I give you a lesson on how to undress a man. Next time you're doing the work."

Julia lay back, her head pillowed on her arms, a sensuous smile curving her full lips. She bent one knee in unconscious invitation and Marc heard the increased pounding of blood in his ears.

"Go ahead, professor, I promise not to take my eyes off you." As if she could, Julia considered as Marc's formal attire fell onto the thick carpeting one piece at a time. His olive-hued skin was tanned to a deep bronze, and her loving gaze followed the jet arrowing of hair over his chest to where it disappeared below his belt.

Marc's gaze was teasingly seductive as he hooked his fingers into his belt loops and slowly lowered his black dress trousers to the floor, stepping out of them. The navy briefs concealed nothing of his desire, and Julia unconsciously pressed her palm atop the increased thudding of her heart as she waited.

"Have you got it so far?" Marc's eyes glinted with a thousand messages, each more provocative than the last.

Julia grinned. "It's indelibly printed onto my memory banks. Carry on."

"Perhaps we should have a quiz on the material presented so far."

Devils of amusement danced in his eyes as he appeared not at all disturbed by the fact that only a scant piece of cotton was between him and the desirable woman stretched out on his bed.

"I don't remember a test being on the schedule," Julia complained softly.

"It's a pop quiz."

He rubbed his long fingers against his dark thighs, apparently in absent thought. The provocative motion drew her attention downward, to the corded muscles of his legs, and Julia decided she'd had enough.

"I've something dreadful to confess, professor," she stated calmly.

His black brow arched inquisitively. "Oh? What's that?"

Julia was on her knees in an instant, her fingers curling around the elastic waistband. "I always cheat on tests."

She yanked the briefs down, letting them drop unheeded to the floor as she basked in the glory of Marc's body. If this is what the men of ancient Italy were like, she thought, no wonder so many had been immortalized in stone and bronze. He was all leashed power and muscle, glistening with a sheen that made him look like a marble statue carved by a Renaissance sculptor. No, she corrected, her eyes drinking in his hard body, that was too cold. Bronze, she decided, dark, gleaming bronze.

Marc needed no further invitation and joined her on the bed, kneeling as he faced her, his thighs pressed against hers, his chest hard against her breasts.

"You realize I can't let you get away with that," he scolded with mock severity.

"Oh, I understand, professor," Julia admitted breathlessly. "I'll take my punishment like a woman." Her eyes were delicate pools of need as they held his gaze. "Whatever do you plan to do with me?"

"I don't know," he admitted, his hand running from her shoulder to her thigh, creating an ache deep within her. "I suppose I'll have to keep you after class while we come up with something."

Julia clung to his shoulders, a soft whimper issuing from her lips as his hand moved to the inside of her thigh, his gentle touch locating her very core. He was pressed against her lower abdomen, alive with shared need, and as his fingers explored the welcoming warmth of her, she shuddered.

He lowered her backward with a gentle force until she was lying prone on the mattress once again. His fingers abandoned their sensual exploration, moving instead to trace erotic circles on her full breasts. The designs grew smaller and smaller, working inward to the full buds, and when he brushed his palms against her taut nipples, Julia moaned softly from the pleasure.

"God, you're magnificent," Marc murmured, his lips moving over her body, tasting every warm pore as she writhed and shuddered under his touch. "You're made for love . . . Look how you come alive at my touch."

His caressing lips and tongue sampled every bit of feminine flesh, locating every sensitive hollow, discovering erogenous zones Julia herself had never known existed. It was incredible; the more he fanned Julia's escalating flames of desire, the higher his own flared. By the time he settled himself between her thighs, nudging at her legs gently with his hands, Marc's body was trembling with agonized need.

"Please, Marc," she gasped finally, her nails raking primitive paths on his back, "please love me, now."

Willingly obeying her desperate request, Marc surged into her. Dazzling colors exploded behind Julia's eyes in a brilliant, dazzling rainbow. Burying his face in her throat, Marc began to move with an age-old rhythm that neither body had forgotten.

Julia moved with him, her satiny legs wrapped around his thighs, absorbing him with a familiarity that erased the years of separation. She felt the tingling sensation spiraling outward, sparking her nerve endings to vivid awareness as she rode the golden spiral to suddenly shatter into a million shards of crystalline brilliance.

"God, you make me feel good," he murmured, his breath fanning her forehead. His fingers traced lazy paths on her body as she lay with him, her head on his shoulder, her legs entwined with his. "You're an incredibly responsive woman, Julia Cassidy."

Julia was still basking in the warm afterglow of their lovemaking and smiled a soft, fulfilled smile.

"You're the only person who's ever made me crazy like that," she admitted, her lips brushing his love-dampened skin.

Marc pressed a soft line of kisses down the side of her cheek. Their lovemaking had swept away the last vestiges of his resentment, and right now he only wanted to spend the rest of his life with her nestled securely in his arms. Her auburn hair fanned across his chest like flames, and he wound his fingers idly through the brilliant strands.

"You were right, Marc," she said in a pleased voice. "It's like nothing ever happened. It's still the same." Her palm rubbed his hair-roughened thigh. "Better."

God, how he wished she hadn't brought it up. Not now. Not here. Marc fought against the poison of bitter memories, reminding himself that she'd changed. But despite his best efforts, his body tensed.

Julia rolled over onto her stomach, looking down into his suddenly shielded dark eyes. "Marc?"

"Dammit, Julia," he groaned, bringing her to him in a crushing embrace. "Why the hell did you have to waste all those years playing stupid games?"

Marc asked himself how could he rail at her for such behavior when he hadn't been totally honest with her. It was time to change that. His dark eyes roamed over her startled features.

"I was telling the truth when I told you I've never stopped thinking about you, Julia. But I have to admit, I've hated you, too."

Her eyes widened at his admission, her complexion losing its soft pink flush as she paled visibly. "Hated me? Why?"

"Because you were so willing to take whatever you wanted, not caring enough to count the casualties afterward."

Her hands shook as she pushed a tumbled cloud of hair out of her eyes. "I was never like that. I'll admit I wanted you and did whatever my silly seventeen-year-old mind could think of to attract you that summer, but I was well aware of the casualties, Marc, since I was one of the walking wounded."

"*You?*" he asked on a harsh note of disbelief. "I fail to see exactly how you suffered, Julia. You stayed in your comfortable home the rest of the summer, traipsed off to a private eastern college, and became a hotshot banker. You came out of the entire fiasco smelling like a rose."

She shook loose of his embrace, sitting up to grasp the sheet against her breasts. Marc lifted a mocking brow at her sudden display of modesty, but Julia ignored it.

"You've got a damn poor memory, Marc. *You're* the one who conveniently skipped town, leaving me alone to face my parents, who, needless to say, weren't at all pleased to discover their only daughter had become a liar and a sneak."

She paused, drawing new breath for her attack. "They could only attribute my rebellion to association with a Castellano. A lot of good your behavior did to my argument that you were someone special!"

"Skipped town?" It was a not very well-muffled roar, and Julia cringed instinctively at the rage vibrating in Marc's deep voice. "Is that what you call it? Hell, I'm surprised you and your father didn't go all the way. A little tar and feathers to dispose of the unsuitable lover!

"You weren't the only one with family trouble, Julia. Let me tell you how much my uncle appreciated your father's little visit." Marc's eyes flashed at the memory. "Especially the sheriff. I've always thought that was a nice touch."

Julia's fingers froze around the sheet, her knuckles turning as white as her face. "What are you talking about?"

Marc returned her intense look, his eyes searching her astonished features. Her eyes were huge and distressed as she stared at him, her shock too great to be feigned. He rubbed his palm over his own face, his moan muffled and indistinct. When he finally removed the trembling hand, his gaze was as bleak as a tomb.

"You didn't know." It wasn't a question.

"Know what?"

Julia jumped as his fist hit the pillow beside her, his fury radiating from every pore. Marc raked his fingers through his hair and left the bed, pacing the room like a caged panther. A terrible thought began to formulate in her mind as he seemed on the verge of murder.

"My father came to your house? With the sheriff?"

Marc stopped at the window, staring for a long, silent time out at the black sky, remembering that night as if it were only yesterday. A shooting star suddenly burned its way across the horizon, snapping him from his bleak thoughts. He answered her in a low, flat voice.

"He did. The two of them were actually quite polite, but eager to remind me that I'd spent the summer taking a seventeen-year-old girl across state lines for immoral purposes." Marc turned to her, his eyes hard as obsidian. "Would you care to know the minimum sentence for that?"

"No," she whispered, knowing that they had both gotten fifteen years. "What happened?"

"The sheriff was understandably uncomfortable, but he was facing a reelection campaign that fall, and your family could always be counted on for a generous contribution."

Marc left unsaid what they both knew. Julia's father had the definite advantage, since Marc's uncle would not have been allowed the same opportunity to buy the lawman's favor. A candidate couldn't be caught accepting money from the Castellanos.

"Your father was very generous." Marc's tone was

acidic, his words bitten off through clenched teeth. "As long as I was willing to leave the county immediately, he wouldn't press charges."

"I understand now why you left," Julia whispered.

"Dammit, Julia, you don't know a thing about it! I didn't agree to leave in order to save my own hide. They could have put me in jail for a hundred years, I wasn't about to leave you willingly!"

"Then, why did you?"

"Your father played his ace. He told me you'd sent him because you were afraid of me. Afraid I'd hurt you if you refused to see me again."

Marc's eyes shadowed with a pain Julia felt in her own heart. "He said you only let me make love to you in the first place because you were too frightened of me and my family to say no."

Despite his apparent acceptance of the fact that she'd known nothing about her father's midnight visit, Julia could detect the question in his last statement.

"Oh, Marc," she whispered, the sheet dropping as she held out her hands to him. "I never felt that way—never. Let me prove it to you."

With a muffled sound that was part groan, part sigh, Marc responded to the golden invitation in her eyes and crossed the room to her outstretched arms.

Julia took a deliciously long time, drawing out every touch, every kiss, until his entire body had been reassured of its appeal to her. Her hands fluttered over him like graceful birds, her lips plucked his burning skin. She teased him, tantalized him, and tortured him with a touch so sweet that Marc was quivering with his need. Her stroking hands asked for forgiveness for past sins, real or imagined, while her tender lips promised a future of delight.

"You're a witch," he gasped as she brought him to the

brink of oblivion time and time again, only to slow the pace until every nerve in both their bodies was strung tight, tremoring for release.

"I hope so," she whispered, her tongue darting out to slowly trace the outline of his upper lip, "because I'm trying awfully hard to cast a spell over you, Marc Castellano."

When Julia's own flaming desires could stand the taunting no longer, she pressed herself against him, intimately adjusting her pliant curves to his hard, muscular strength. Marc's hips left the mattress as he thrust upward, his body seized by its own demands now as he moved to make them one.

She sheathed him in her warmth as he filled her completely, their lovemaking seeming endless as they sought to make up for the years so cruelly stolen from them. It was as if neither could get enough of the other, each meeting in a passion as uncontainable as a wildfire blazing across a parched, open prairie. Much, much later, exhausted, but finally satiated, they collapsed into a deep sleep.

When Julia first awakened, she was confused by the strange surroundings. Then she remembered, and a full, satisfied smile curved her lips as she stretched her arms above her head in sheer pleasure. She could hear sounds from downstairs, and rose from the bed, anxious to join Marc. One glance at the beaded gold dress hung over a chair reminded her that she had nothing to put on. She couldn't show up at the breakfast table stark-naked, even if the idea was undeniably tempting.

Practicality winning out, she located a royal-blue robe in the closet and slipped it on, tying the sash tightly about her waist. She went downstairs, wondering at the fact that she knew exactly where the kitchen was. As she reached the doorway, it struck her.

"This is our house!"

Marc turned, looking every inch the successful businessman in a dark flannel suit.

"Good morning to you, too," he greeted her with a smile.

"Now I know why it seemed so familiar last night. You built it from our plans."

Marc handed her a glass of orange juice as well as a teasing grin. "You call those scribblings you did on tattered scraps of paper plans? It's a good thing you're a banker and not an architect, lady."

"Answer me, Marc Castellano." Julia felt like an absolute idiot as she stamped her foot.

"Not until I get a good-morning kiss," he murmured, drawing her into his arms and covering her lips with a warm, leisurely touch. "Aah. That's a much better way to start the day, don't you think?"

"Perfect," she agreed breathlessly, slipping her hands beneath his gray suit jacket, stroking his back in a sensual invitation.

"A witch," he said with a soft chuckle. "But I'm afraid we don't have time for that, sweetheart. You're overdue at the bank and I've got an early flight."

"You're leaving?" Julia's face fell.

"Just for a few days." Marc put his fingers under her chin, lifting her distressed gaze to his. "I'll be back as soon as I determine what the hell happened at Apollo. It's a sensitive system they may have stolen, honey. The fallout could be disastrous."

Julia sighed, wondering a bit guiltily how she could have possibly forgotten Marc's problems. She kissed him tenderly, deciding that when you were so well and expertly loved, it was difficult to think of anything else.

"Well, I suppose I'll have to let you go, then. But I won't like it."

She sipped her juice, watching warily as he prepared breakfast, frying lean strips of bacon and eggs, keeping them warm on a hot plate while he toasted the bread. Julia was not a big fan of breakfast and had to instruct her stomach to behave as the scents assailed her nose. She dragged her gaze from the platter, stifling a sigh.

"You did design this house from the plans we drew that summer, didn't you?"

"Of course."

Had he built it with her in mind? Had he always considered living in it with her? Had he pictured the two of them married, teaching their children to swim in the lake? The image was an appealing one, and as she sipped the coffee he placed before her, along with the unordered breakfast, Julia allowed herself to get carried away with her domestic fantasy.

She fit so perfectly into this room, this house, Marc thought as he sat down across the table. But that was not really any surprise. Despite the fact that he'd fought to keep his resentment of her simmering all these years, this morning he was able to admit he'd built this house for her.

His love for Julia Cassidy had gone into every board, his need for her into every brick. He'd designed the bright, cheery kitchen with the vision of the two of them sharing breakfast, as they were right now, watching the dawn paint the eastern sky a delicate rose color. The den was designed for working at home, and he'd wandered idly around the room during construction, imagining Julia's auburn hair illuminated to a gleaming copper by the fat yellow bars of afternoon sunshine.

He'd let his fantasies run rampant in the bathroom, driving the architect to distraction on more than one occasion as he supervised every detail of the sumptuously erotic room. And the bedroom . . . The construction of the loft bedroom had brought more pain than pleasure as he'd relived those stolen hours of lovemaking. Including that disastrous last time . . .

But they'd managed to overcome the past, and right now it was all he could do to keep himself from doublebolting the door, not freeing her until she agreed to marry him. But Julia had matured into an intelligent, independent woman who'd undoubtedly refuse to accept such Neanderthal tactics. As hard as it was, Marc decided to move their relationship along slowly, giving her a chance to get used to the idea.

"Marc?" Her soft voice broke into his thoughts.

"Yeah, honey?"

"Why did you come back?"

"To move Apollo headquarters to Reno. You heard me tell Uncle Joe how much I love this place." Marc hesitated a heartbeat of a moment, trying to decide whether to continue. "And, to be perfectly honest, since that seems to be the rules of the game this time, I wanted to show the locals. You know, bad boy makes good, that sort of thing . . .

"I'm damned successful, all on my own. And I like to think certain individuals will be made aware of that every time they drive by Apollo corporate headquarters."

There was one thing more, but Marc felt uneasy about relating the ridiculous scheme to her now. For years it had seemed to be exactly what he'd wanted, a goal he'd never let out of sight. This morning he felt he no longer knew that embittered, vengeful man. In fact, if he were to die right now, he'd go a happy man for having been to heaven last night.

"Oh." Julia could understand both those reasons, but she'd been hoping for more. "That's all, then?"

He put his fork down and picked up his coffee cup, taking a long drink, buying time. His eyes were somber as they looked at her and she realized the question had been a difficult one.

God, he was going to take a chance on her understanding and tell her, he realized. "Truth?"

Julia nodded, folding her hands in her lap so he wouldn't see them trembling. "Truth," she whispered.

"I also returned for revenge, Julia. I wanted to hurt you as badly as you hurt me." At the look of wounded shock on her face, he hastened to continue. "But I think I knew as soon as I entered your office that I'd never be able to do it. Because I cared for you too deeply."

"You must have hated me terribly."

"I tried," he admitted, his black eyes not leaving her anguished hazel ones. "How about you?"

"I tried, too."

"And?"

"I couldn't."

He gave a short nod, his lips drawn firmly together for a moment. "I know the feeling very well. Think it's time to bury the hatchet?"

She gave him a wobbly smile, her hand leaving her lap to take the one he'd extended across the table. Their fingers linked together, his dark and hers fair, pledging a new beginning.

"I'd say it's time," she agreed.

They ate in comfortable silence, Julia doing her best with the meal, not wanting to hurt Marc's feelings after he'd risen early to prepare it. Enjoying this shared time together, Marc was not eager to return to the real world. But it was time. He forced his mind back to practicalities.

"You can have a pair of my jeans and a shirt to wear home," he said. "They won't fit very well, but at least it'll keep you decent. We certainly can't take you directly to the bank in that little number you wore last night." He gave her a pleasant leer as he rubbed his jaw thoughtfully. "Of course, that might not be such a bad idea. Just think what it'd do to bring in new accounts."

"Silverado Fidelity has a very conservative image," Julia retorted with a wide smile.

Marc failed to return the smile, his expression turning suddenly serious. "I realize that. What do you think they're going to do about one of their executive officers living with the infamous nephew of a gambling-establishment owner?"

"What?"

"I want you to move in here as soon as I get back from Palo Alto," he said calmly. "Actually, I'd prefer you move in today, but I don't have time to teach you all of SAM's idiosyncrasies. I wouldn't want you to end up accidentally turning on the automatic sprinkler system and flooding us out."

He spoke about it so casually, she mused, as if there were not a doubt in his brilliant mind that she would hesitate. Oh, Julia wanted to spend the rest of her life with Marc Castellano, but she'd woken up this morning with marriage on her mind. It had never occurred to her that he wouldn't be prepared to offer that.

But he was offering her everything else, she reminded herself. And this time, she was going to take whatever she could get. The alternative was too painful.

"I'll be packed and waiting," she promised, her eyes warm with love as they met his watchful gaze.

Chapter Nine

The somber faces worn by the key members of Marc's staff revealed they shared Brian Huhn's concern that he hadn't returned last night.

Last night. The very thought of making love to Julia brought a smile to his firm lips. He stared out the heavily tinted window to the northeast for a moment, wishing he was back at Lake Tahoe. Only a harsh whisper from Brian jerked his mind back to reality, and heaving a deep sigh of resignation, Marc returned his attention to the problem of his software theft.

"Are we going to withdraw the program? After all the money we've already invested?" Jordan Mathison, financial wizard for Apollo Enterprises, had been covering a legal pad with figures continuously during the meeting.

"I don't know yet, Jordan."

"Money isn't always the most important thing," Brian snapped as he met Jordan's challenging gaze across the table.

"Try telling that to MIT when you're out of a job and can't make your kids' tuition payments," Jordan countered. "If you were allowed your way, Huhn, Apollo would have gone bankrupt years ago."

Jordan and Brian were poles apart when it came to the

financing for new projects, as well they should be, Marc thought. Brian was brilliant; his imagination pushed against the barriers of reality, creating today what was impossible yesterday, all while working on new frontiers for tomorrow. The other side of the coin, Jordan, was methodical and prudent. Jordan's often-thankless task was to keep Brian from spending every cent the company earned on what were often controversial projects. The two men complemented each other perfectly, even if their difference in temperaments made these meetings less than cordial.

"We're all here to decide what we're going to do," Marc reminded them both. "Fortunately, the system hasn't been installed yet, so let's not get ahead of ourselves. This is going to be a rough-enough day without unnecessary arguments."

"The rest of us were here last night." This pointed observation was offered by Johnny O'Keefe, the only man in the room who'd dare to use such a tone with Marc Castellano.

Marc shook his head with reluctant chagrin. Johnny had taught him just about everything he knew about computers and the computer business. The stubborn old man refused to come into the business, despite repeated offers of a full partnership. He preferred instead to remain at Cal Poly, readily available whenever Marc needed an expert consultant. Since Johnny had no financial interest in Apollo and no reputation to protect, his views would be the most unbiased of all.

"I know that, Johnny. And I appreciate you coming on such short notice."

The gray head laced with several rust strands bobbed agreeably. "I'm here for the duration, Marc." He cleared his throat as his worried light-blue eyes met Marc's. "You know, you've got a hell of a problem we haven't brought up."

"Time. Every minute that goes by, we're that much closer to having the theft exposed. Something that could easily ruin our otherwise spotless reputation."

Johnny's mouth was set in a grim line. "It could put a shadow over all your projects. Especially the top-secret government ones."

Marc had known that last night. But at the time it hadn't really mattered. Not as much as being with Julia. He shook his head at his own uncharacteristic behavior. Now he had to get this mess straightened out in time to save Apollo. If he was going to be a family man, he had certain responsibilities.

"Let me suggest this," he decided. "Since the program hasn't been implemented, we'll notify the ABA member banks to keep a close eye on all transactions. If a break-in occurs in the next few days, it'll probably be a hacker, easily tracked down by the FBI computer experts."

He left unsaid what everyone knew: if nothing showed up for several weeks, it would point toward organized crime. The system would have to be altered considerably, costing both time and money, as well as doing irreparable damage to Apollo's reputation. Jordan was visibly relieved at the decision, but Brian, as expected, began to lobby for a new program.

Marc was able to escape the renewed argument of the two men when the FBI agents arrived to begin their investigation. He led them to personnel, promising to join them shortly. He had one important call to make.

"Hello?" The soft, breathless note in her voice thrilled him, temporarily lifting the burden from his shoulders.

"Hi, yourself."

"Oh, Marc, what a nice surprise! Would you believe that I was just thinking about you?"

Lord, that lush voice could warm his blood even across long-distance lines. "That's what you're supposed to do. Think about me. And all the ways I'm going to make love to you when I get back."

"How is it?" she asked, genuinely concerned. He sounded so tired.

Marc considered telling her about the EFT program, then decided it could be taken care of when the warnings went out to the member banks. He damn well didn't want to waste their time talking about business.

"It's been hell around here, honey. You can't imagine. But in the middle of chaos, I realized I don't know how I'm going to survive being away from you. Here I am, facing a problem that's got even the hard-core atheists muttering Hail Marys and I'm acting like a lovesick kid. Can you believe it?"

"I can," she whispered into the phone, twirling the cord around her fingers. "Because I'm going through the same thing here, Marc. I miss you."

"And I miss you, babe," he responded somewhat absently as Johnny opened the door.

"You'd better get down to the lab, Marc. Those feds are going through the place like a damn hurricane."

"Marc? Do you have time to tell me what's happening there?"

"I can't right now, honey. In fact, I've got to get back. I just wanted you to know that last night meant the world to me. *You* mean the world to me."

Julia's words of love were cut off as Marc said a quick good-bye and broke the connection. She was still staring at the receiver, wishing she could call him back when Charles entered her office.

"I can't believe it."

"Believe what?" she asked, lowering the receiver to its

cradle. Her gaze shifted to Charles as he settled into the chair across her desk.

He flipped a newspaper onto the desk. "Page eighteen. 'All Around Town.' "

Julia searched out the gossip column that added daily spice to the society page, a lump growing in her throat when she read the description of her evening with Marc at the Castellano casino. Short of direct libel, the innuendos were undeniably damaging.

"As usual, they've got their facts wrong," she said calmly. "The wine was a lovely California chardonnay, not French champagne, and we shared a bottle, not a magnum."

Charles wasn't amused. "Since when do you gamble?"

Julia struggled to hold her temper, trying to maintain the golden feeling Marc's call had brought. She took her time arranging papers on her desk, lining them up with all the precision of a NATO general reviewing the troops.

"Since last night. I thought it was time."

"How much did you lose?"

Julia couldn't help the runaway grin. She'd lived in Reno long enough to know that runs like hers were uncommon, almost miraculous, which was one reason she had enough sense not to repeat last night's performance. But she saw no reason to tell any of that to Charles.

"Actually, I won."

His eyes narrowed in speculation, his gaze suddenly shrewd. "How much?"

"Enough," Julia answered easily, her broad grin widening to reach her eyes.

"I think it's damn unreasonable of you to criticize my gambling habits, then go out and play roulette all night," he complained. "Besides, I could have used your lucky streak myself."

She arched her delicate brows over the frame of her glasses. "Oh? Was it that bad?"

"It wasn't good," he acknowledged, rising from the chair with a smooth, masculine grace. "I don't suppose you'd loan me a bit of your winnings, just to tide things over."

They had been through this before. Julia had loaned Charles money innumerable times, never again seeing a penny of it. Lately she'd joined with those who'd given up supporting his gambling habit.

"I'm sorry, Charles." The contrition in her soft denial was genuine. Julia was honestly sympathetic, but didn't feel that contributing to his weakness would help him overcome it.

"Forget it," he said brusquely. "It wasn't that much and I'm coming into some money soon that'll pay it off, with interest."

"Oh? Have you latched on to a big account? Or did some long-lost relative die?" She added the last as a jest, hoping to dispel the odd anger she'd seen wash across his features.

Charles turned in the doorway, a half-smile playing about the corners of his mouth. "Something like that," he responded inscrutably, leaving the room. Julia heard the light laughter from outside the door, a sure sign he'd returned to normal and was flirting harmlessly with Marge.

She didn't give a great deal of thought to Charles' assured prediction. He was constantly promising new and wonderful accounts that always seemed to fall through at the last minute. Obviously he'd met someone at the game last night who'd halfheartedly agreed to discuss bringing his business to Silverado. Julia hoped this one would prove more successful than the others.

*   *   *

Marc rinsed his face in the sink, raising bleary eyes to the mirror. At least he looked as bad as he felt, he considered, eyeing his red-rimmed eyes and stubbled jaw. They'd been at it for hours, and if any of the men still at work in the conference room stepped out onto the well-swept streets of Palo Alto, they'd probably be arrested for vagrancy.

He'd discarded his tie and vest long ago and unfastened the top two buttons of his shirt. Marc scowled as he saw a single gray hair interspersed amid the black. He'd probably have a hell of a lot more before this was over, he thought bleakly. His shirt looked as though he'd been living in it a week, and he could smell the cigarette smoke embedded in the fibers of his clothing. And Johnny O'Keefe's god-awful cigars . . . Marc made a mental note to have his secretary buy the man a box of decent Havanas. They'd have to be an improvement over whatever those things were he was smoking now.

Exhausted, he needed to hear a friendly voice. Ignoring the hour, he slipped away into a private office.

"Hello?" The soft voice betrayed her disorientation.

"I woke you." He knew he would. It was an incredibly selfish thing to do, but, Lord, how he needed her.

"No, you didn't. My mind was somewhere else," Julia lied, hugging the receiver closer to her ear as if she could lessen the distance between Palo Alto and Reno.

Marc leaned back against the wall and shut his eyes, practically seeing her slender hands as she pushed the sleep-tumbled hair out of her eyes.

"Where?" he challenged softly, the first hint of laughter he'd felt all day lacing his voice.

"Where what?" Julia was still struggling to wake up.

"Your mind," he reminded her patiently. "You said it was somewhere else. Where was it?"

"Oh, that." She laughed, a silvery, merry sound that

lifted him momentarily from his exhaustion. "It was lost in my dreams," she admitted. "What time is it, anyway?"

"Too late. But I was lonely . . . Were they good dreams?"

She laughed again, this time a throaty, provocative sound. "Let's just say I wasn't lonely," she teased lightly. "I think that was why I had such a hard time understanding what in the world you were doing on my telephone when you'd been doing such amazing things right here in my bed."

Erotic images flashed behind his own lids as he sank into a swivel chair and closed his eyes. "That bad, huh?"

"Or that good, depending on how you look at it." Her voice held a definite smile. Then she focused on a clock. "Good heavens, Marc. Are you still working? At this hour?"

"Still at it. But I'm playing hookey to talk to my lady."

"You poor man. Do you want to tell me about it?"

"When I get back home and can laugh about the entire thing," he decided. "Why don't you tell me about your day, instead?"

Julia arranged her pillows as she sat up. "Well, when I finally arrived at the bank, it was as if I'd set off a siren."

He put his feet up on the desk, leaning back in the chair, his eyes still closed as he idly played with the telephone cord. Just hearing her soft voice was like a sedative and Marc found himself relaxing for the first time in hours.

"Hmm. Is it that unusual for the officious Ms. Cassidy to be late?"

"Of course it is," she answered briskly. "But that wasn't the reason. We made the paper, Marc. The 'All Around Town' column."

His feet hit the floor. Damn. That was all they needed. He'd hoped to have some time before their relationship was forced to stand up to public scrutiny. "I'm afraid to ask what it says."

"Let me read it to you," she suggested. Julia clicked on the lamp and ruffled through the newspaper. "Here it is . . . 'Banker Bets All on Spin of Wheel.' " Her voice was calm as she read the article to him.

"I'm sorry, Julia. I never meant that to happen when I insisted on going to the casino."

"Oh, it gets even better," she assured him. "Listen how he closes: 'We can only hope it was her own money our reckless gambler was throwing around like rice at a Sicilian wedding. Because I doubt the customers of Silverado Fidelity Bank would consider a roulette wheel a safe investment.'

"I was amazed at how many people read that trash. Charles gave me the paper in the first place. Then I dropped into the executive lounge for a cup of coffee and conversation ground to an absolute halt. Even Dad called."

Marc rubbed his face with his hand. Well, it had been a nice pipe dream, he thought bleakly. Now that James Cassidy was back in the picture, he may as well kiss his future with Julia good-bye.

"Marc? Are you still there?"

"Huh? Yeah, honey, I was just wondering what you told your father."

"I told him that since he was the lawyer, he could figure out how to sue Ron Cunningham for that slander."

"Is that all?"

"No."

Marc groaned as he stared out at the glow of pink on the eastern horizon signaling the approaching dawn.

"Look, Julia, I'm dead on my feet out here, miles from the woman I love. Could you be a bit more informative rather than making me drag the story from you bit by agonizing bit?"

"I'm sorry, darling. I shouldn't have teased you like that . . . I said I'd been out with you. Then I advised him not to bother with the sheriff this time because I'm a grown woman and intend to cross that state line every chance I get."

Marc felt as if ten tons and at least a thousand years had just been lifted from his shoulders. He leaned back in the chair, his feet back on the polished surface of the desk.

"Thank you, sweetheart. Believe me, I'll reward you for that little act of bravery as soon as I get home."

"I'll hold you to that promise, Mr. Castellano," she said, her silken voice provocatively husky.

"Tell me about the rest of your day. It sounds as bad as mine."

"I'm sure it wasn't," she countered quickly. "But there were a fair share of opinions offered. Want to hear my mother's?"

"I can't wait," Marc returned dryly.

"She's decided that since you're moving Apollo's home office to Reno, you need the one last thing that will show everyone you've finally made it: a suitable bride."

"Respectability by marriage."

"That's it. Aren't you clever? Who would have thought you and my mother would ever think alike?"

Her teasing tone was meant to take away any pain Betsy Cassidy's accusation might have once caused, and Marc chuckled with a reluctant good humor.

"Any other well-meaning souls offer their advice to the fallen woman?"

"Well, George said it was great. But you know, I have a sneaking suspicion he's been doing some matchmaking all along. I think that's why he refused to let me off your account."

"That's part of the reason," Marc admitted blandly. "So, you're confessing you wanted off?"

"Long ago, when I wasn't nearly so clever," she responded absently, her mind obviously on something else.

"Three days is such a long time?"

Julia laughed. "I'm a fast learner. Wait a minute! You said matchmaking was *part* of George's reason to hold me to Apollo. What was the rest of it?"

"Can't you guess? An intelligent, fast learner like yourself?"

"Why, Marc Castellano, you used sexual politics to select a bank. That's horrible!" Julia was both amazed he'd do such a thing, and pleased she actually meant that much to him.

"Hey, you're good, sweetheart, but I do have the livelihood of eight thousand employees to consider. Selecting your bank was purely a business decision, although I'll admit to asking George to throw you in to sweeten the pot."

"I'm not sure I'm thrilled about the idea of being some pawn in this game you were playing, Marc."

He sighed wearily. "Julia, try to look at it reasonably. You're happy the way things turned out, aren't you?"

"Well, yes."

"And if you'd been given the choice, would you have worked with me on my account?"

"No," she admitted softly. "Not on a bet."

"And we both know you don't bet. So, you see, darling," he crooned into the receiver, "I was just trying to save us both any more lost time. We've wasted enough, Julia."

It was the solemnity with which he spoke her name that convinced her. She gave a slight, resigned sigh.

"I understand. But don't expect to get away with such

behavior on a regular basis, Marc Castellano. This is going to be a fifty-fifty relationship."

"Fifty-fifty," he agreed. "Speaking of that, have you decided what to do with your share of the winnings?"

"Yes, I'm donating it to the Make A Wish Foundation. I know you told me to use it for myself, but I'll really feel better giving it to those children. Besides, I'm so lucky, Marc. I already have everything I want. I've got you."

"Do you know how much I want to be there with you? Right now?" His voice was a husky growl.

"Not as much as I want you here. I don't think I'll ever be able to sleep alone again."

He laughed. "Just work at it, sweetheart. There will be hell to pay if I come back unexpectedly and discover Charles Stevenson keeping my side of the bed warm."

"Oh, pooh," she scoffed. "That was never serious, and you know it. He asked me to loan him some of my money, by the way. After giving me a rather tart lecture about gambling in the first place."

Marc's mind suddenly brought forth a mental image of Jack Murphy's cluttered home. As the principal designer of the EFT software, the man had been the most logical suspect. When Marc had accompanied the FBI to the man's house, he'd been stunned at what they found. Computer hardware and electronic gear had filled several of the rooms, and five antennas occupied the roof. All the clothes had been removed from the closets, but the bitter odor of burned coffee suggested the man had left in a hurry. He'd forgotten to turn off the coffee maker and the liquid had caramelized in the bottom of the Pyrex carafe.

A few items had been inadvertently left behind, and the FBI agents had slipped them into plastic bags. There were what appeared to be journals, written in some sort of mathematical code that they'd set the computers to work deciphering, and Julia's story about Charles Stevenson made Marc recall the tip sheets scattered about the den, indicating Murphy played the ponies.

"Did you give him any?"

Her sad, rippling little sigh told its own story. "Not this time."

"What did he say to that?"

"That was kind of funny. I really expected him to hit the ceiling. Or at least mope for the rest of the day. But he didn't seem to care. He said something about coming into some money that'll pay off all his debts with interest."

Julia frowned as she speculated on Charles' behavior. "I hope this one pans out. Poor Charles, he's always promising George that he's going to bring in a new and wonderful account, but it always seems to fall through at the last minute."

Marc couldn't feel sorry for the guy. He was a firm believer in the fact that the cards usually fell exactly the way you stacked them. Charles Stevenson had been born with a full house. It was his own doing that had made them fall down around him.

He was saved from commenting by a brief knock on the closed door, a signal that they'd begun once again. "Julia, I've got to go. Take care of yourself. I'll be back as soon as I can."

"Good night, Marc. Please try to get some sleep," she advised with little hope that she could influence his working decisions. "I miss you."

"I miss you, too. And you can take that to the bank, lady."

Julia smiled as she replaced the receiver and snuggled back down under the covers, returning to her dreams of Marc's wonderful lovemaking.

*   *   *

When ten days passed without another word from him except a daily delivery of long-stemmed roses, Julia was forced to wonder if she'd been too hasty in her decision to move in with Marc. At the time, unhappy about the lost years they could never regain, she'd been willing to settle for what he was offering.

But his recent behavior made her wonder how happy she'd be, living with a man who couldn't give her a total commitment. If he loved her, wouldn't he want to marry her? The terrible thought that he'd returned only to avenge himself tickled her mind. What if he'd only wanted to seduce her, then drop her, in order to cause her the pain he'd suffered over the years? What if he had no intention of ever returning to the Reno-Lake Tahoe area?

No, her banker's mind retaliated, don't forget that tall mirrored tower you pass every morning on the way to work. Apollo is definitely moving here.

But that doesn't necessarily mean Marc has any intention of furthering your relationship, the uncertain woman within her reminded the banker.

The insistent jangling of the telephone shattered Julia's restless sleep. Attempting to focus on the green digital numbers of her clock radio, she wondered who would be calling her in the middle of the night. The middle of the morning, she corrected, eyeing the three-fifteen inches from her nose.

"Hello?"

"Hi. This is the Castellano moving company. I'm calling to see when the lady of the house will be ready for our truck."

She sat up in bed, shaking tumbled hair from her face as she gripped the receiver with both hands. "Marc? Do you have any idea what time it is?"

"Hi, honey. I'm sorry I woke you, but I just got in and I couldn't wait to hear your voice. It's damn lonely around here; SAM isn't nearly the company he used to be. I think he's depressed."

For the sake of peace, Julia decided not to point out that he'd had ten days to hear her voice. They had telephones in Silicon Valley, after all.

"A depressed computer? Come on, Marc, how many drinks did you have on your flight from Palo Alto?"

"Not enough to forget you, sexy lady. And yes, I do believe he's depressed. He misses a certain gorgeous lady banker who smells of sandalwood, jasmine, and flowers . . . So do I."

"I've missed you, too, Marc. For the last ten days."

Marc had turned his back on Johnny O'Keefe's advice to get some sleep before taking the corporate jet back to Nevada in the middle of the night. He'd had to get home to Julia. He wanted to be with her when she found out about the theft. Exhausted as he was, he caught the sarcasm edging her words.

"I'm sorry about not calling, honey. Did you get the flowers?"

She glanced at the petals scattered about the base of the tall vase holding the first day's roses. When she'd realized they were going to be a daily occurrence, she'd instructed the florist to deliver them to a local nursing home, rationalizing that someone should get some enjoyment from them.

The once-velvety petals of the delicate Peace roses were brown and withered, but Julia hadn't found the strength to throw them out. They were her only link with Marc, her only proof that the entire reunion hadn't been a dream.

"I did," she answered his question finally. "Thank you. They died."

"You're mad at me."

"No, I'm not mad, Marc."

"Good." His deep voice still held a hint of concern, but she could tell he'd decided not to try to discern her problem for the moment. "What time do you want to move?"

"Marc, I've got a full schedule today. I didn't expect you back." The words fell out in a rush and she closed her eyes, leaning back against the pillow, waiting for his argument.

"Oh."

Through her closed lids, Julia could see Marc pondering the problem, long fingers rubbing his square, thrusting jaw, deep horizontal furrows marring his brow. His dark eyes would be narrowed, those ridiculously long, curly lashes making shadows against his high cheekbones.

"I should have called you. To make arrangements," he decided.

"You should have called me," Julia agreed.

"How about this evening after work? I can bring over a pizza and help you pack."

"I'm busy this evening," Julia lied poorly, her eyes still tightly shut as she garnered strength to carry through with her decision.

"I see." His cool tones indicated that Marc was, indeed, catching her drift. Fatigue made him impatient. "I realize you don't have your appointment book with you in bed, Julia. Even *you* aren't that devoted to business." She flinched at his sharp words. "But do you happen to recall a time in the next forty-eight hours when you can move in with me?"

Julia shook her head on the pillow, a single tear escaping her lid, the gesture doing nothing over the telephone lines.

"Julia? Are you still there?"

"Yes . . . no . . . I mean, yes, I'm still here and, no, I don't have any free time."

"Do you envision any free time this week?" he pressed her, his voice hardening further.

"No . . . I'm sorry, Marc."

"Not as sorry as I am, Julia. I'm damn sorry I bothered you."

"It was no bother. I'm glad you called." She really was. She'd been aching to hear his voice, praying constantly for days that the phone would ring. But pain always overcame pleasure where Marc Castellano was concerned, it seemed.

"Oh, I can tell, sweetheart. You're just tickled pink. By the way, I talked to your boss before I left Palo Alto. The three of us have a breakfast meeting this morning at seven."

"Seven? Marc, that won't give you any sleep," she protested.

"So what else is new? See you there."

Marc slammed the phone down and Julia pressed the receiver to her cheek for a long, long time, knowing that she'd done the right thing. The only thing she could have possibly done. But she wondered why the proper behavior made her feel so rotten.

She loved Marc, but she didn't want the crumbs of his life. She wanted to be a full, intricate part of it. She longed to share the bad times with him as well as the good. That had been the problem nagging at her the past ten days. She knew, when she hadn't heard from him, that things had to be bad at Apollo. Yet he hadn't seen fit to share his problems with her.

Never, in all those days, had he considered picking up a phone and calling her for advice or comfort. No, Marc Castellano obviously considered her comforting abilities to be purely physical.

Julia wasn't the only one who found the long-awaited telephone call less than pleasurable. Marc belatedly realized he'd made an error in judgment. Although he'd been working around the clock, there had been times he longed to pick up the telephone and call her, seeking comfort from her soft, calm voice. But each day had only brought worse news. Deciding the best thing to do was to get things finished up as quickly and efficiently as possible so he could return to her free of this overwhelming problem, he'd sent the flowers so she'd know she'd been continually in his thoughts.

He spent the predawn hours preparing the information for his meeting with the FBI, thinking that the entire episode was unbelievably coincidental. It pestered his logical mind, disturbing his thoughts, and now he had the additional burden of wondering whether Julia would believe him innocent when she discovered that her beloved Silverado Fidelity Bank had lost ten million dollars to his software system.

Chapter Ten

Marc was employing all his negotiation skills, Julia noted, eyeing her watch for the umpteenth time, wondering how late he planned to be for their meeting. As it was, she'd smoked her way through half a pack of cigarettes. She lit another, groaning as she realized she already had one burning in the ashtray.

"I'm sorry I'm late."

As if conjured up by some genie of her thought process, Marc was suddenly standing in the doorway. Julia stared, unable to believe this was the same man she'd last seen over a breakfast table less than two weeks ago. His dark eyes were ringed with purple shadows, like deep bruises, and his handsomely chiseled face was drawn, his cheeks sunken. His dark complexion was an unhealthy shade of pewter gray, suggesting a current life-style of not enough sleep and a poor diet. She struggled to hide her dismay.

"That's all right," she assured him, rising from behind her desk to greet him. "George is late, too. It's a little ironic, actually."

"What's ironic?"

Marc leaned against the door frame, still not entering

the room. His hands were jammed into the front pockets of his navy slacks as he eyed her with curiosity.

"I'm the one who hates breakfast, yet I'm the only one on time."

"You hate breakfast?"

"I detest eating anything before noon," she admitted.

His dark eyes widened with honest confusion. "But you ate my breakfast that morning."

He looks awful, Julia told herself. At least give the man something nice to remember. She admitted to herself that she'd handled it badly, yet wasn't quite ready for such an open confession. She gave him an uncertain half smile.

"Overwhelmed by your charms, I didn't want to turn down anything you were offering."

"But you ended up doing exactly that," Marc reminded her. "Unless you've changed your mind in the last few hours."

He felt like shaking her as she detoured the subject blithely, her voice briskly professional. "I've got your file in order. It really amazes me what you've done in such a short time, Marc. You should be incredibly proud."

"I love that dress. It reminds me of a soft summer cloud."

Julia ran her palms down the powder-blue cashmere sweater dress, unnerved by the light gleaming in Marc's tired eyes.

"Thank you. Now about your file—"

"You look different. Softer."

Julia fought the pink flush that betrayed her pleasure in his words. "You look different, too," she answered pointedly.

Marc groaned, finally leaving the doorway to sink into a russet leather chair, stretching his long legs out in front of him. He eyed the toes of his shoes for a long, silent time.

"The last ten days have been hell."

"I'm sorry."

He lifted his gaze to hers. "Are you?"

Julia felt like withering before the piercing stare and lit yet another cigarette. "Of course I am. What in the world do you take me for?"

Marc laced his fingers together behind his head, leaning back to eye her with ill-concealed mockery. "A smart woman such as yourself should know better than to ask a loaded question like that, Julia Cassidy."

"Why do you do this?" she asked in a soft, tremulous tone.

"Do what?"

"Go out of your way to show me how little I mean to you. Not to mention dangling Apollo Enterprises out like a juicy plum while you're luring me into your bed."

She watched him rub his slightly stubbled chin. He'd obviously worked all night, not even taking time to shave before coming here. She longed to hold him in her arms and soothe away whatever cares and woes Apollo was causing him. But by his silence on that score he'd effectively told her his desire for her had nothing to do with sharing anything but his bed.

"Let's just say you're like Mount Everest, Julia."

"Mount Everest?" She lifted one delicate brow above the frames of her glasses, inviting him to elaborate.

"You know, if it's there . . ."

Julia stabbed the cigarette into an ashtray, breaking the unsmoked part in half with the vicious gesture. "You've no idea how that flatters me, Marc. To be compared to yet another one of man's challenges."

His square jaw thrust out a little farther, appearing even more chiseled in its unkempt state, and that telltale muscle jerked along his cheekbone, demonstrating the tension lying under the surface. "It wasn't meant to be flattering," he stated brusquely. He pushed back his cuff to look at his watch. "When do you think Stevenson's going to show up? I've got another appointment at nine."

"With another bank?" While she'd tried to keep the anxiety from her voice, Julia knew he had heard it by the way his eyes hardened.

"Don't fret about your commission, sweetheart; it's not with another bank. It's with the FBI, as a matter of fact."

Julia paled instinctively, and Marc jerked, raking his fingers through his hair in obvious frustration.

"You never really change, do you, Julia? What's the matter now? Are you afraid your nice little bank will have to launder some of Marc Castellano's gambling funds?"

She was struggling to come up with an answer to his harsh accusation when George showed up, followed by Charles. The older man appeared, if possible, even worse than Marc. His silvery hair was ruffled, as if he'd been combing his fingers through its lush strands. His eyes showed the strain he was feeling and every line in his tanned face sagged with exhaustion.

"George, what's wrong?" Julia raced to his side.

"The EFT," he said, his expression grim. "They got us for ten million dollars, Julia. The discrepancy showed up in last week's audit. Ten million dollars, broken down into little bits of electronic data, left the Federal Reserve and never showed up here. It's vanished into thin air."

Julia sank into her chair. She shut her eyes to the whirling dizziness accompanying George's unwelcome news.

"Castellano." Charles' triumphant proclamation sounded almost pleased as he glared across the room at Marc.

"That's ridiculous," Julia snapped.

"No it isn't. It's obvious."

"Charles, shut up," Julia insisted, glancing nervously in Marc's direction.

Marc surprised Julia by how little the accusation appeared to disturb him. He shrugged his shoulders in a weary gesture.

"Let him talk, Julia. This might prove the first amusing moment I've had in days."

Julia continued to glare at Charles as he ticked off his distorted facts on long, tapered fingers. "Number one, the guy suddenly shows up on Silverado's doorstep, claiming an interest in opening an account. Two, ten million dollars mysteriously disappears from the EFT on its way here. Three, as you've so often pointed out, Julia, our 'customer' just happens to be a computer genius." Charles nodded, his mouth set in a grim but self-satisfied smile. "Castellano's our man."

Marc watched the color rise in Julia's cheeks as she fought a battle with that Irish temper he knew she still possessed. He remained silent, eyeing her with admiration as she chilled her gaze to hazel ice.

Her fingers had unconsciously curled around a crystal paperweight, and from the cold fury in her eyes, Marc would not have been at all surprised to see it headed toward Stevenson's blond head.

"That's ridiculous," she said, white lines circling her tight lips. "You're ridiculous, Charles."

There was a smothered sound from George, the unsuccessfully stifled response somewhere between a gasp and a laugh.

"And what's wrong with my deduction?" Charles retorted.

He appeared quite sure of himself and Julia realized she'd always hated the way he could be so smug. For someone so inept at functioning in the world that had been created for him, Charles was gifted with incredible self-confidence.

Everything's wrong with your stupid deduction, she wanted to screech. I love Marc Castellano. And I could never love a man who'd do something like this. Never.

"Marc?" She looked over at him for confirmation, but he only gave her a crooked half-smile.

"You're the one who got the free science lecture, Julia. I'd enjoy seeing if it took." He nodded, encouraging her to continue.

Julia dragged her eyes away from his warm gaze, forcing her mind to draw a parallel between this conversation and the one she and Marc had shared in the restaurant parking lot.

"The problem with your reasoning, Charles, is that the accuracy of deductive logic depends on the validity of the principles. Your data is way off; you're taking two totally unrelated incidents and forcing them together like mismatched jigsaw puzzle pieces, just in order to come up with the big picture. But you're wrong and it's wrong."

"You still haven't pointed out the error, Julia," Charles stated, his palms on her desk as he leaned toward her. "What do you have to go on, except the fact that you're infatuated with the guy?"

Julia wondered if Charles was jealous about losing her to Marc Castellano or if he was simply jealous because Marc embodied everything George Stevenson held dear, while it was readily apparent that George's feelings for his only son were less than admiring. She looked over to George for encouragement. Surely he didn't think Marc would do this?

"George?"

The older man nodded his tousled silver head. "You're doing fine, Julia."

"Fine?" Charles protested in a voice resembling a whine. "She still hasn't come up with one concrete reason why the FBI shouldn't be marching in here to arrest Castellano."

"All right, Charles," she sighed. "In the first place, you're right about Marc being intelligent. He's brilliant, but even a criminal with the IQ of a mushroom would realize that stealing the money from our bank, when he's spending so much time here, would be stupid. It's so obvious, it's overkill."

Her eyes moved to Marc's face, sweeping over his ravaged features with a warm, intimate message that made him decide all this trouble might be worthwhile, after all.

"And in the second place," she continued, her gaze slowly returning to Charles, "I know the man. I have to go with my instincts. He didn't do this."

"I know about your instincts," the younger Stevenson ground out, having seen the look of love that passed between Julia and Marc. "I suppose now you're going to tell me that you never gave Castellano our code while the two of you were sharing a little pillow talk?"

As Julia blanched at the accusation, Marc pushed himself up from the chair, looking as if he'd enjoy pushing Charles Stevenson through the nearest wall.

"Apologize for that, Stevenson, or you'll find out just how primitive a man with generations of Sicilian blood flowing through his veins can be." His long fingers curled into threatening fists at his sides as the air radiated with a furious energy.

Charles wisely decided not to put Marc to the test. "I didn't mean it, Julia. I know you've always been a loyal employee." He said it with the air of the aristocracy speaking down to a peasant, but watching the muscle jerking in Marc's jaw, Julia decided it would be prudent behavior to accept the apology, weak as it was.

"I'm going to forget you even suggested such a vile thing," she returned aloofly.

"Well, that's that," Marc said with deliberate nonchalance. He nodded brusquely, then marched across the thick carpeting in long strides, turning in the doorway, his expression shuttered.

"I'll be in touch." He was down the hallway before she could get around her desk.

"Marc—"

Winter was threatening, the sky a heavy slate blanket that matched the asphalt parking lot. Julia caught up with Marc as he reached his car, her breath shallow from running down the stairs instead of waiting for the elevator. He spun around at her words, his face resembling a thundercloud.

"Damn it, Julia, it's thirty degrees out here. What do you think you're doing without a coat?"

"You didn't give me any time," she retorted. "And let me tell you, Marc Castellano, I'm sick and tired of you walking out on me. So knock it off. Do you hear me?"

To her amazement, Marc threw back his head and roared, the laughter coming from deep in his chest. "I hear you, Irish."

He shrugged out of his jacket, placing it around her shoulders. The flash of warmth she felt at his touch had nothing to do with the heavy material.

"You're driving me crazy, Julia. Despite all the problems I've got, you still possess the capability of throwing me for a complete loop. Do you realize how many people have accused me of outright arrogance? Of possessing an ego that would make Napoleon look like Mr. Milquetoast?"

Julia hugged Marc's jacket to her. "I can imagine."

"And do you realize that every bit of that arrogance

flies out the window when I'm with you? You devastate every little bit of self-esteem I possess."

Despite his attempt at control, Marc grasped her by the lapels, pulling her nearer. "A few minutes with you, Julia Cassidy, and I'm no longer Marc Castellano, computer entrepreneur, but Marco, the kid who delivered booze to your restricted country club."

"Oh, Marc."

Julia breathed a soft, regretful sigh and gave into her instincts, reaching up to brush her palm along his cheek. His dark beard felt like sandpaper as she cupped either side of his face with her hands. Her lips caressed his with a slow, sensual pattern as she pressed her body against him. After a long, delicious interlude, Julia slowly backed away.

"I love you, Marc. And I'd love you whatever your name or circumstances of birth." She bent to pick up the coat that had fallen to the ground, handing it to him. Then she turned to leave.

"Julia?"

"Yes?" She glanced back over her shoulder.

"Send over whatever papers are necessary. You've got Apollo's account. We'll hash over the details later, all right? After I get a bath, some sleep, and a couple of decent meals under my belt."

She nodded, her behavior matching his solemnity, knowing they had the rest of their lives to settle their personal problems. "I'll have Marge send them over to your temporary office by messenger this afternoon," she promised. "Or should I have them delivered to the house?"

"The office will be fine. Someone there can bring them out to me if I've gone home."

"That's a good idea, you know."

"What's a good idea?"

"Going home to bed. You honestly look awful, Marc."

Julia watched his face sag. "I honestly feel awful, honey." He folded his long length into the sports car and drove away as Julia returned to the bank building.

Charles had disappeared, but George was waiting for Julia as she returned to her office. She rubbed briskly at her arms, attempting to stimulate the flow of blood to her chilled body. Why was it that, in Marc's presence, she hadn't felt the chill at all? By the way her body had responded to his nearness, it could have been summer. But now she could barely feel the tips of her fingers and her toes were blocks of ice in her suede shoes.

"What do we do now?" she asked softly, lighting a cigarette. She stared out over the rooftops of Reno as if she could spot the ten million dollars floating free somewhere.

"There's nothing to do except wait. The bank examiners are going over the books now. Hopefully, we'll be able to track the diversion."

She nodded, staring out at the highway that led to the lake.

"Julia?"

"Hmmm?" she answered absently, straining to see if she could find Marc's black Lotus in the swirling snow.

"Get out of here. He needs you more than I do right now."

Julia went over to the older man, kissing him on the cheek. "Thank you," she whispered. She walked to the brass rack, taking down her coat and shrugging into it.

"Oh, and Julia?"

She turned in the doorway, looking back over her shoulder. "Yes, George?"

"Tell Marc I appreciate all his help on this. Assisting the FBI in tracking down our computer thief, when he's up to his neck in his own trouble, is above and beyond the call."

The snow fell in sparkling wet flakes that stuck to the roadway under the tires of Julia's car. She'd forgotten to have the snow tires put on the Colt and was paying for it as she drove the winding road to the California side of the lake. The wind picked up, driving the wet snow against her windshield, piling the flakes up with a speed that made it difficult for her worn-out wipers to keep her vision clear. Julia mentally lashed out at that odd quirk in her memory that failed to retain the necessities of everyday life. Why hadn't she at least remembered to replace those wipers?

She inched along, her top speed twenty miles per hour as the familiar drive seemed like a trek into uncharted Antarctica. The soft white snow muffled the sound of her tires on the gravel of his driveway, and as Julia walked to the door, she practiced any number of opening lines, none of which sounded remotely natural to her ear.

The door opened as if by magic once again, and as she entered the sunken living room, Julia heard a whirring and the oddly humanoid voice. "Hello, Ms. Cassidy."

"Hi, SAM. Where's your boss?" Julia responded as she momentarily forgot SAM was nothing but a computer with more brains than average. She realized her folly as the single camera eye stared at her unblinkingly.

"Dumb," she muttered. "The man has you talking with machines. Next you'll be asking the vacuum cleaner how its weekend went."

She climbed the stairs and stood in the bedroom door, observing Marc as he slept. He looked as though he'd fought the Hundred Years' War single handedly, but as he lay on his back, one hand flung above his head, he reminded her of a sleeping child.

Without the slightest hesitation, Julia stripped down

to her bikini panties and slid under the sheet, snuggling up against Marc's hard, warm body.

"Mmm. Julia? Is that really you?" Marc's dark eyes fluttered open, his pupils wide and dilated as he tried to focus his bleary vision on the face only inches from his own.

Smiling a greeting, Julia brushed her lips lightly against his, the kiss a tender pledge. "It's me, darling," she affirmed gently. "Go back to sleep, Marc. I'll be here when you wake up."

"I've missed you, Juliet. God, how I've missed you. Promise me you won't leave?"

"I won't leave, Marc," she whispered, taking him into her arms. "I promise. Sleep now."

"I love you, Juliet."

Marc's ebony lashes rested on his cheeks as he drifted back into his peaceful slumber, leaving Julia to stare in thoughtful wonder. Did he mean that? Did he really love her as she loved him? She wanted to concentrate on that idea, to consider the glorious possibility. But Julia had not been sleeping well herself during Marc's absence, and the comfort she found now, lying with him in the wide bed, drew her to sleep as well.

Her hand brushed at the lazy tickling along her thighs, coming into immediate contact with another hand, stronger and wider than her own. Her eyes flew open, meeting Marc's amused gaze as he stared down at her with unashamed affection.

"I honestly thought you were a dream until I woke up. It's still taken me the last half-hour to believe my good fortune."

Julia pushed back some tumbled hair from her forehead. "You've been watching me sleep for half an hour?"

"Uh huh."

She squirmed slightly under his melted-chocolate glance. "That's not fair."

He grinned, the smile incredibly boyish. "Of course it's fair. How long did you watch me before you decided to take the plunge and join me in this bed?"

"Awhile," she admitted. "But I couldn't help it. You looked so . . ."

"Sexy?" The grin turned absolutely provocative.

"No, not really . . . although your body looked great, the way your chest rose and fell with your deep breathing." Julia placed her palms on the pelt of dark fur, her fingers teasing his skin. "It's a very nice chest."

"I'm pleased to hear I live up to your strict standards. Then I was at least moderately desirable?"

"Not really." Her hazel eyes sparkled with amusement, golden imps dancing at his obvious dig for a compliment.

"Then what the hell do I look like when I sleep?"

"Like a little boy. I wanted to hold you in my arms and take care of you, so no one could ever harm you," she answered honestly.

"Damn. Remind me never to fall asleep in front of you again, sweetheart. That's not the image I've been working on. I wanted to inflame your passions, not stimulate your maternal instincts."

Julia laughed. "You do that quite admirably, too, Marc. In fact, I was sorely tempted to take advantage of you right then and there. You were saved only by your obvious exhaustion."

"I'm not exhausted now," Marc murmured, his palm stroking the soft skin at the inside of her thighs.

Julia gasped at the thrill that shot along her veins at his feathery touch. She tried to tell herself this was not what she'd come here for. She'd planned to discuss the theft and assure him that she'd never, for a single instant, questioned his innocence.

But as his tracing fingers trailed sensuous paths over her body, bringing every inch to vibrant life, Julia admitted that this, too, was why she'd driven that dangerous path to Marc's remote home. She'd been aching for his touch, his kiss, his exquisite lovemaking.

Her own hands moved down the solid planes of his chest, across the firm abdomen that revealed long hours of exercise, over the crisp, curly jet hairs no longer concealed by his briefs.

"Oh, Marc . . ." Julia rained soft kisses over his skin. Smooth skin. He'd obviously been up long enough to shave.

"You planned this," she complained lightly as she stroked his cheek and inhaled the tangy scent of his after-shave.

"Of course." Marc's hands shaped her firm calves, his long fingers massaging gently as he worked his way up her legs. He could feel the wanting coming off her in waves, and as his fingers dipped into the warm, welcoming softness, Julia gasped.

His warm breath feathered a path down the axis of her body, and when his lips and tongue replaced the practiced finger, she cried out, thrusting her hands through his dark hair. His caresses were unrelenting in their intimacy as he led her higher and higher, to where the air grew thinner with every sensual stroke.

This was the way he wanted her today, he realized instinctively. She'd scored a direct hit to his ego when she'd remained so aloof and serene in her office. But the woman trembling under his touch was vulnerable as she opened herself to him. Marc felt a primitive surge of exaltation at the sweet sound of her soft cries.

"Marc . . . please." Pent-up longing thickened her

voice as Julia's head tossed on the pillow, her thick auburn hair spread out like tongues of golden-red flames.

"Please what, honey?" he asked as he continued making love to her.

Please what? Did she honestly want him to stop this exquisite torment? Unable to answer, Julia allowed her body to speak for her, her slender back arching off the sheets as she moved into his wonderful lips.

Marc's deep chuckle rumbled, like a tide breaking on a distant shore, as his hands and mouth continued to lead her up the steep, unfamiliar mountainside until Julia was poised at the summit, tottering precariously on the brink of oblivion.

"My God . . . oh, Marc . . ." Her head thrashed on the pillow, every nerve in her body stretched as she struggled to maintain her last grip on sanity.

"Go ahead, sweetheart. Let it go, Julia . . . relax and enjoy it."

Relax? How could she relax when her body was rigid, every nerve ending focused on that one explosive part of her body? Then, when she thought she would surely shatter from anticipation, Julia toppled off her jagged peak, crying out Marc's name as her fingernails dug into his muscular shoulders. She clung to him desperately as she fell, landing into the safety of a lush, soft meadow with a shuddering release.

"I love you, Juliet," he murmured, his hands tangling in her hair as he let the coppery strands sift through his fingers.

"I love you, too," she murmured. "So much."

"I know. You proved that today."

"Today?"

"When you attacked that idiot Stevenson; I felt adored, actually." His grin was wide and self-satisfied.

"Oh, you haven't seen anything yet, darling," she

murmured, extracting herself from his embrace to rise on her knees beside him, her hair a fiery waterfall as it skimmed his body.

Her hands began to move, lightly at first, then with more authority as she demonstrated the veracity of her claim. Her lips caressed him with increasing boldness, causing his body to tremble under her intimate touch. Now it was Julia who was intent on conquest, and Marc realized he'd misjudged her once again. This was no soft, submissive woman surrendering to his masculine needs because she lacked the strength to control her own desires. This was a woman bent on seduction. In a blinding flash she'd become Eve, Salome, Delilah—every female who'd ever brazenly taken her pleasure from a man.

"God, woman, you're driving me wild," Marc groaned, his fingers tangling in her flaming hair as he moved his hips, establishing a rhythm she followed for a time.

"Love me, Julia. I need you, sweetheart . . . I need all of you."

Julia sensed the quickening of his body and slowed the pace in much the same way he'd done for her, drawing out each sensation so he could derive the fullest possible enjoyment. She knew his rumbled protests were as false as her own had been, and when she finally led him to his own mountain spire, her heart soared at the pleasure she derived from his ragged cry.

"Oh, Julia." He shook his head, his dark eyes glazed with emotion as they moved over her flushed face. God, she was beautiful. "You always were a vixen."

She laughed, a silvery musical sound, as they shared memories that were not all painful. "Only with you. You bring out something very elemental in me, Marc. You always have."

"You always were a naughty wench," Marc teased her, his lips brushing along her cheekbone, nibbling at her warm skin.

"You didn't really want me that summer, did you, Marc?" she murmured, shutting her eyes as his lips brushed butterfly kisses on her lids.

He punctuated his answer with short, hard kisses. "Of course I did. Couldn't you tell?"

"But you kept ignoring me."

When he lifted his head, Marc's eyes were strangely serious. "I was doing my best to avoid temptation, Julia. You were young and spoiled, and I didn't think you had the slightest idea what you were doing, sending out signals like that. I was four years older and figured it was up to me to keep things from getting out of hand.

"I knew that if I were alone with you for one minute, I'd end up doing what I'd been dreaming about ever since I'd first seen you, a wide-eyed innocent who'd just gotten her first jolt of desire. For a stranger. And a forbidden one at that . . . Then there was the fact that your father would just as soon have me tarred and feathered as not. Face it, honey, the entire scenario was explosive as hell."

"I know," she sighed. Julia didn't want to think about the sad times and she let her hazel eyes wander around the cozy interior of Marc's bedroom.

"I really adore this house."

"I'm glad. It would've been damn ironic if I'd built it to your specifications and you changed your tastes over the years."

Julia returned Marc's smile. "Nothing about my taste has changed over the years, Marc. In houses or in men."

He laced their fingers together, lifting her wrist to a tender kiss. Marc's smoky gaze moved from her soft, love-lit eyes, down over her slender frame, along the smooth expanse of creamy thigh. He wondered momentarily about the severity of the season's first storm, which was blowing snow against the windows, and hoped it would set new records. He never wanted to move from this spot.

"I wonder how long this storm's going to last." Julia's question echoed his own thoughts, and Marc shrugged.

"I don't know. Even if it stopped snowing right now, it'd probably be tomorrow before the roads are plowed."

Julia sighed, wishing it would never stop snowing. The soft sound was misinterpreted by Marc.

"I'm sorry about this, honey. But there's nothing we can do but wait it out."

Her fingers smoothed at the furrows on his brow with gentle strokes. "That's not it. I was just hoping for the granddaddy of all storms."

Marc's ebony brows arched, his eyes bright with hope. "Really?"

Julia's hazel eyes sparkled up at him; her lips grazed his cheeks. "Really," she confirmed with a bold, feminine smile that had Marc drawing her into his arms once more.

Chapter Eleven

❧

Mother Nature seemed to be conspiring with the two lovers: the snow continued for three more days. The tension dissolved from their relationship and Marc and Julia spent the time making up for the lost years; long hours of conversation were punctuated by rapturous lovemaking. Julia soon felt as if she'd lived in this house forever. Even SAM seemed like a longtime friend.

"I tell you, you're making him too human," Marc teased as Julia congratulated the computer on the preparation of dinner. "He's programmed to operate the microwave, honey. It's no big deal."

Julia took a bite of the stew that had been a colorful, frozen lump when they'd gone upstairs to the bedroom.

"All I know, Marc, is that this is the most delicious meal I've ever eaten. I sure didn't cook it, and you were too busy showing off your exquisite lovemaking talents to be concerned with culinary projects. If it wasn't for SAM, we'd be eating this meal with ice picks. I don't know how I ever got along without him."

Marc grinned. "Perhaps I should be jealous."

Julia put down her fork with a slow, deliberate motion. The warmth her look generated could have melted all the drifted snow that had fallen thus far. "Don't be, Marc.

There's one thing you do to perfection that no computer could ever be programmed to achieve. If I had to choose only one of you, darling, you'd win out every time."

"Are you suggesting we forgo dessert?" His ebony eyes danced with pleasant lust. "SAM's baked a cherry pie just for you."

Julia rose from the table, extending a slim hand down to Marc. "I'm sure it's delicious," she acknowledged, "but maybe SAM should keep it warm for a while."

"A while? That's not in his program," Marc protested. "If you're going to be living with him, Julia, you've got to learn to be more specific."

Her smile was beatific. "Tell him we'll have the pie for breakfast."

Marc tried the phones off and on during their snowbound holiday, but the lines had apparently fallen from the heavy snow.

"You're worried." Julia looked up from her solitaire game, her gaze sweeping over his face with concern.

"Guilty," he admitted on a self-deprecating grin. "Wouldn't you think that any man snowbound with a gorgeous, luscious female would have enough sense not to keep trying to reach the outside world?" He crossed the room, massaging her shoulders as he stood behind her chair.

"It's only natural to worry, Marc. I'll admit to having more than a passing interest in what's happening. Ten million dollars isn't small change. Even in the investment-banking business."

He reached past her, putting a red six on a black seven. "They're related, you know."

Julia turned up the three of spades, which she placed onto the four of hearts. "What's related?"

"Your computer crime and my software theft. I know they're done by the same guy."

That was what Charles had insisted. Surely Marc couldn't mean . . . ? Julia shook her head. Of course Marc wasn't about to tell her he'd masterminded the theft. Where did she get these crazy ideas, anyway?

"What makes you think that?" she asked in a voice she wished was steadier.

"Do you think I'm the crook?" he asked bluntly.

"Of course not," Julia responded instantly.

"But the coincidence does disturb you," Marc pressed, his voice low and neutral.

She stared at the cards, refusing to meet his probing gaze. Marc's tone made her extremely uncomfortable. "Certainly not. Life is full of coincidences, Marc. If we worried about all of them, we'd never have a moment's peace."

"If you're not upset," he argued, "then why did you just put that eight of diamonds onto the seven of hearts?"

She glared up at him. "Damn it, Marc, we can't all have minds that function like computers. All right, this entire subject makes me nervous. But not for the reason you're thinking."

Her hazel eyes handed him a warning. Don't press, it cautioned. Please, it's been so lovely, don't ruin it now.

Marc ignored the silent advice. "Why do you find it so upsetting, if you don't still harbor some doubt about my possible gambling ties?"

"Damn it, Marc, that's it!" Julia flung the deck of cards to the table, scattering several of them onto the floor. She pushed back her chair with a loud scraping sound, tilting her head to meet his steady dark gaze. Her slim hands were balled into fists on her hips, the gesture tugging at the material of his shirt she wore, exposing an even longer length of creamy white thigh. It was all Marc could do to keep his mind on this conversation.

"Listen to me, Marc Castellano, you may be the

world's smartest computer genius, but you're an absolute washout when it comes to understanding anything about a woman in love. I worry about you, you big dope."

Her finger jabbed at his chest. "When I hear people like Charles Stevenson jump so quickly to conclusions, I have to wonder if anyone else is thinking you're involved in that crime. Especially since you haven't seen fit to discuss it with *me*."

"I didn't want to disturb you with my problems," he retorted. "How the hell was I to know that *my* program was going to intercept funds on the way to *your* bank? The odds against that happening were astronomical!"

Julia snorted, an unfeminine, disbelieving sound. "You didn't want to worry me?" Her voice rose several octaves. "You didn't think it had anything to do with my bank? What makes you think I only operate as a banker, Marc?

"I didn't spend the time you were in Palo Alto worrying about my damn bank. I was going crazy worrying about what was happening in your life. I was also incredibly hurt to realize you didn't care enough about me to share your troubles. All you seemed interested in was a warm bed on both sides of the state line!"

Marc's eyes expanded with surprise as he watched the fiery woman whose eyes were just beginning to brim with hot tears. Tears of anger, he realized. And frustration. Damn. She was right. He'd been an absolute idiot.

He reached out to cup her shoulders with his palms, but Julia backed away, shaking her head. Her thick hair swirled between them, a fluffy auburn cloud.

"Not this time, Marc. You can't get out of this discussion by making love to me. I want to settle this once and for all."

Marc dropped his hands impotently to his sides. He picked up her cigarette pack from the table, shaking one out and placing it between taut lips. Almost as an after-thought, he tilted the pack in her direction. Julia nodded, accepting the cigarette he offered. The harsh scraping of a match being struck was the only sound in the heavy, expectant silence of the room.

"All right. Do I get a chance for defense, or has the prosecution more evidence to present?" he asked finally.

Julia viewed him warily. It was definitely not in Marc's nature to be so submissive. Her hazel eyes swept across his features, searching a sign. But his dark gaze was shut-tered.

"Go ahead." She nodded brusquely.

"Are we allowed to sit down or is this a stand-up bat-tle?"

"You sit on the couch," she decided. "I'll sit over here."

Julia chose a chair across from him, not trusting Marc enough to share the couch. Sex had been a most persua-sive argument in their relationship and she was deter-mined not to give him that edge.

Marc watched Julia settle into the plaid wing chair with all the manner of a deposed Russian empress. It was amazing how regal she was able to appear, clad simply in his faded black and silver Raiders T-shirt. Her long legs, crossed at the knees, seemed to extend forever. He sighed.

"I'll admit to not calling you while I was in Palo Alto," he said. "I will also admit to underestimating the extent you'd matured over the past years. My only defense in that matter is that I love you and didn't want you upset. The young girl I'd once known would not have handled my problems well." He drew in on the cigarette, eyeing her appraisingly. "I failed to give the woman the credit she was due."

His smooth tone rolled over her, admiration and regret

n every word. Julia knew she was going to forgive him. But she remained silent, encouraging him to continue.

"You already know I've been working on a new encrypting system for the American Banking Association. As you pointed out, Julia, the hardware to encrypt even a single ATM can add five thousand dollars to its cost. Multiply that times the number of automatic tellers in this country and I understand why you bankers have been reluctant to safeguard your systems. The cost of protecting electronic money is astronomical."

He eyed the shortened cigarette thoughtfully for a moment, choosing his words carefully as he felt her silent resistance and sought to answer her objection.

"Granted, ATM thefts don't amount to more than fifty or a hundred dollars at a pop. However, anyone sophisticated enough to gain access to the ATM lines could gain access to the EFT. Now you're talking big bucks. As you've already found out."

Julia accepted his point. "Tell me about your system," she suggested softly.

"It's not that different from the ones we developed a few years back for the ATM, but one flaw we found in our old system is that the sixty-four-bit numeral key we were using to scramble and unscramble the information can become known."

That was the code, the information Charles had accused Julia of giving to Marc while in bed with him, she remembered, a flare of anger reasserting itself at the unpleasant memory. Marc caught the emotion and looked momentarily wary, but when she remained silent, he continued.

"The new system utilizes a more sophisticated system that generates secret keys at random. The goal is to have every member bank of the Federal Reserve encrypted in three years. It also has a message authentication standard that enables participants to know immediately when a line has been tapped."

"And not have to wait for an audit to turn up the discrepancy," she murmured.

"That's right, but your theft occurred faster than we expected. After all, the system isn't even in use yet. Unfortunately, the software gave the crook a working knowledge of EFT."

"But why Silverado?" she groaned.

Marc shrugged. "You know what Willie Sutton used to say, honey."

"Yeah. He robbed banks because that's where the money was. . . . I never believed you had anything to do with this, Marc. Not even for a minute. It's important you believe that."

His dark eyes warmed. "I know. Is this argument over yet?"

Julia's full lips curved into an inviting smile. "Why? Do you want to kiss and make up?"

Marc gave her a lazy, devastating grin. "That's a beginning," he promised. "Then we'll go from there."

"I never knew building snowmen could be such an erotic pastime," Julia declared the next afternoon. "Although I still think you should have given up your scarf, Marc. He looked so naked out there."

Marc grinned as he entered the master bathroom, handing her a tall mug of Irish coffee. "Ah, but he's with his snowlady, so that's the best way for him to be."

Her smile extended to her eyes, warm and reminiscent. "I suppose so. You know, of all the rooms in this house, I love this one best."

She was immersed in the sunken red tub, clad in bubbles, and Marc arched his brows in a friendly, lustful manner. "That's handy, because of all the rooms in the house, this is the one I love you in the best."

Almost every possible luxury had been incorporated into the design as Marc had allowed erotic fantasies of Julia to run free. The ceiling slanted upward, banks of soft lights hidden by imported wood beams. One wall was triple-paned glass and looked out onto the forest. The secluded nature of the two-acre lot enabled Julia to luxuriate in the churning water, surrounded by leafy green plants as she watched the deer gathering at the salt lick outside. A flock of birds had taken possession of the pine feeder, dropping errant seeds to the pheasants waiting below. It was difficult to believe that the glitter of gambling casinos was a short forty-five minutes away.

"I think I could become quite lazy, living like this." Her tongue gathered in the fluffy white cream that resembled the iridescent bubbles covering her.

"Are you telling me you're no longer the obsessive investment banker who drove all the way out here to deliver a contract?" Amusement threaded his voice.

"You know very well I didn't come out here for that," Julia replied calmly, refusing to rise to his suggestive bait. "That contract could have been delivered by any one of a dozen messenger services."

"Ah, but I thought I'd already told you that I prefer a bank with personalized service."

"The only way I could get more personal is to invite you in here with me, Marc. And even that wouldn't be a first."

The severity of the storm, which had continued for a fourth day with undiminished energy, had undoubtedly caused havoc all over the area. But to Julia and Marc, it had brought a blissful respite from the outside world, and she knew she'd always consider these days the best of her life. Today the sun had come out, signaling that their stolen time together was at a premium.

The warm gleam in Marc's dark eyes was mirrored in Julia's own inviting gaze and she waited with anticipation for him to join her under the sheet of bubbles. As he began to unbutton his wool shirt, an alien sound shattered the expectant silence.

"I liked the old system better," he groaned, shaking his head and rising from his knees beside the tub. "Ma Bell would've had far better manners than to interrupt at a time like this. Four days without a phone and it has to ring just when I've come up with a terrific idea of what to do with that whipped cream."

Julia sighed, placing the tall crystal mug onto the wood decking surrounding the sunken tub, and rose to wrap herself in one of the thick towels.

Marc was still holding the receiver as he turned to stare at her, taking in her complexion, flushed from the warm water. Her hair, sparked with ruby lights, had tumbled over shoulders, which gleamed a milky pearl, giving her an aura of ethereal loveliness. He knew her air of fragility was deceptive and hoped Julia wouldn't be too devastated by the news.

"It was Johnny O'Keefe, honey. He called to tell me they located the money."

Julia nodded, not understanding Marc's solemn face. He'd told her of his longtime friend. It was not unexpected that he'd be the one to give the news to Marc. So why was he looking at her as if her nearest relative had just died?

"Marc?" She placed her hand on his arm. "What's wrong?"

Marc's fingers cupped her chin, lifting her confused hazel gaze to his. "You have to understand this comes directly from the FBI, Julia. It isn't mere speculation on Johnny's part."

"I understand that. Now, what aren't you telling me?"

"It was Charles."

She paled. "I don't believe it. Are you saying Charles stole your program? And the ten million dollars?"

He nodded, his mouth a grim line.

"Marc, that's impossible! Charles isn't smart enough to do anything that complicated."

"Charles has already admitted everything to the FBI, honey. He'd gotten himself into some bad gambling debts and was offered a chance to wipe out his markers by giving someone Silverado's ATM code. But he got the bright idea to go them one better."

"I don't understand." Julia's face mirrored her confusion.

Marc's lips tightened into a grim line. "It occurred to Charles that if he went for the big time, the EFT, he could pay off his debts as well as have enough to live in comfort for the rest of his life."

"But how did he get your system?"

"Simple. He read about my work in your files, then flew to Palo Alto, where he offered one of my designers a piece of the action. Stevenson and Murphy had met at a high-stakes game a while back and were both desperate to pay off some pretty heavy gambling debts. With that software and Charles' access to the Silverado computer, they were able to make a clean sweep."

"But the money . . . where is it? Ten million dollars isn't small change, Marc."

"Remember, it's all electronic and it's zapped through telephone lines these days. The ten million was broken down into smaller bits and deposited into various accounts in randomly selected banks in Chicago, Miami, and New York.

"From there, Charles had his share deposited in a secret account in Georgetown. The Bahamian banks aren't subject to scrutiny by the U.S. government, so he planned to spend the rest of his days in tropical luxury. Our storm threw him a curve. The airport was shut down and he couldn't get out of the country fast enough.

"The feds found Murphy boarding a night flight to Rio and he crumbled, admitting everything. Including his collaboration with Stevenson."

Julia sagged down onto the bed, shaking her head with honest regret. "Poor Charles. Poor George." Her eyes widened. "My God, George! We've got to get to him; he shouldn't be alone right now."

Marc gathered her into his arms. "There's a helicopter on its way to pick us up and take us to Carson City. I told Johnny you'd want to be there with George."

She looked up at Marc, giving him a wobbly smile. "You're a good man, Marc Castellano."

He winked a dark eye. "I run around with a pretty classy lady. Some of it is bound to rub off." He ran his finger along the top of the towel, expelling a soft sigh of resignation. "I suppose we'd better get dressed, sweetheart, before the helicopter pilot arrives to discover one ravished redhead lying in the arms of a blissfully satiated man."

Julia divided her time during the next two days between the bank examiners and George Stevenson, offering what comfort she could. Marc had been closeted with the FBI, and their time together had been limited to brief snatches of conversation caught over coffee in the federal office building cafeteria.

She was standing outside those offices, waiting for the cab she'd called to take her back to the hotel, when a long black limousine pulled up to the curb. As Julia curiously peered into the heavily tinted windows, the door flew open and long fingers reached out to grasp her wrist, pulling her into the backseat.

Her sounds of startled protest were promptly silenced by blissfully recognizable lips as she stared into Marc's dark eyes. He reached out, brushing her lashes shut as he covered her lips once again in a slow, sensual kiss.

"What are you doing here?" she asked when they finally came up for air.

"Orchestrating a kidnapping."

"That's a federal offense. Don't tell me you've gotten so chummy with those FBI guys they'll let you get away with such behavior."

"Of course. After all my help in tracking down that money, they're more than willing to look the other way."

The smile faded from Julia's face. "Poor Charles. He never was very lucky."

"I'd say he came out pretty well. It's sure not as bad as it could have been, honey. If Silverado had decided to press charges, he'd be playing his poker games in a federal prison."

"They didn't want the theft to become common knowledge, Marc. Think what that could do to the bank's reputation."

He nodded, his lips pressed into a firm line. "That's what usually happens. One of these days your profession is going to have to crack down on these guys. Pretending computer crime isn't an everyday occurrence is like giving the thieves the keys to your vaults."

"I know." She sighed, adjusting herself to fit into his arms as she tucked her feet underneath her on the wide seat. "But he did give the FBI the names of the men who'd approached him about giving the code to them in the first place. And he's getting help with his problem.

He's agreed to counseling and went to his first Gamblers' Anonymous meeting last night."

"That's a start," Marc agreed. "I *was* surprised that the board of directors is letting him stay on at the bank, though."

A small smile played across her lips. "That's because three out of five voting members of the board are Stevensons," she confessed. "That was a stipulation when the charter was established over a hundred years ago. Besides, he's not going to be allowed to handle any money. George is going to put him in charge of public relations. He's always been good at that."

"I know you grew up with the guy, Julia, but I hope you don't mind that I didn't invite him to our party this evening. I just can't feel too friendly toward him after the mess he's caused for both of us."

"Party? But I haven't seen you alone for two days, Marc." Her fingers played suggestively with the buttons on his shirt.

"We'll have days and days for that, sweetheart."

"I have to be back to work tomorrow," she reminded him.

"No you don't. SAM called you in sick." Marc took the glasses off her face, folded the stems, and slipped them into an inside jacket pocket.

"SAM? Don't tell me you've got him moonlighting as a female impersonator these days?"

"Not exactly." His finger traced the delicate line of her jaw, moving up to drape her hair behind her ears. "I surreptitiously recorded some of our phone conversations while I was stuck with the FBI and you were spending all your time with those bank examiners. Then, after a little judicious editing, I taught Sam the proper responses to the questions most likely asked by your switchboard operator." Marc grinned. "It was a cinch, actually."

Julia stared up at him. "Are you telling me that you not only illegally taped telephone conversations in front of agents from two federal agencies, you also made SAM an accessory to a kidnapping?"

Marc shrugged uncaringly. "SAM's safe enough. He's programmed to erase his own memory banks if arrested."

"That's very clever," she said, pressing a light kiss against his smiling mouth.

"I thought so." Marc plucked at the fullness of her warm lips, leaving a trail of kisses from one corner to the other. God, how he loved her. "I got the idea from an old James Bond movie, actually," he tacked on with a casualness he was far from feeling.

"Really?"

"Sure. It's like a spy swallowing a cyanide pill. But in SAM's case, the suicide is even more terminal."

Julia cringed. "That pun is criminal in itself, Marc." She sighed happily, her gaze filled with a warm promise. "Do you really think anyone would miss us, Marc? Couldn't I tempt you into skipping this party for one of our own?"

Julia was surprised as Marc groaned and shook his head. "I'm afraid we've got a full house, honey. I guess my kidnapping plans leave a little to be desired on that score."

"A full house?"

"Let's see . . . there's Johnny O'Keefe, Brian Huhn from research, and some other people from Apollo."

Her face fell a bit, but her smile only wavered at the corners of her lips. "Oh. Is it a business function?"

"Of course not." Marc continued to name the guests. "The three FBI guys will be there, too. They insisted on an invitation, since they're supplying the transportation. This is their limousine," he explained at her questioning look.

For the first time since he'd yanked her into the car,

Marc's eyes expressed his uncertainty. "Then, I hope you don't mind, but I invited my uncle."

Julia grinned. "Of course not. It'll give me a chance to show him I've learned how to brew a proper cup of coffee. Maybe that'll convince him I'm good enough for his nephew."

Marc returned her smile, the flush of pleasure brightening his face. "You're a terrific woman, Julia." His next words were overtly casual. "Oh, and we can't leave out your mother—or your father."

Julia's hazel eyes widened as she stared up at him. "Do they know your uncle is going to be there?"

"Of course. I wouldn't pull a dirty trick like that." Marc eyed her with gentle disapproval.

Julia reached up and patted his cheek. "Of course you wouldn't, darling," she soothed. "But I have to admit that if you've actually managed to get our families together in the same room without threats of murder or mayhem, there's nothing else you could do that would ever surprise me."

Marc watched her face carefully, dropping his bombshell in a casual tone.

"Then, of course, there's Father Kavanagh."

"Father Kavanagh?"

"It's best to invite the priest to the wedding ceremony, darling," he replied blandly.

"Wedding?"

His ebony head nodded. "Wedding. I know you're not a big one for gambling, and I can see where you might consider marriage with a hardheaded computer scientist a gamble, so I wanted to give you time to get used to the idea. . . . But you've been driving me crazy, Julia Cassidy, and I'm not going to accept a single complaint or excuse. Is that clear?"

Marc's jaw thrust forward as he looked down at her

with an expression that brooked no refusal. But inside, he was holding his breath and he knew his heart had stopped beating.

Julia struggled to keep the breakaway grin from claiming her face. Her expression remained casually nonchalant.

"Well?" His deep baritone voice held impatience.

"Well, what?" Julia inquired sweetly.

"Well, what the hell do you have to say about it?"

Her smile broke free, blinding in its dazzling light as she flung her arms around his neck, pressing a blizzard of kisses all over his face.

"I'd say, Marc Castellano, that you're jumping to conclusions again, accusing me of underestimating the odds. Our love is no gamble, my darling. In fact, I'm so sure of winning this time, I'll bet the rest of my life on it."